RIVALS IN LOVE AND WAR

DAN O'SULLIVAN

CRANTHORPE
MILLNER
PUBLISHERS

First published by Cranthorpe Millner Publishers (2024)

ISBN 978-1-80378-187-7 (Paperback)

www.cranthorpemillner.com

Cranthorpe Millner Publishers

Printed and bound by CPI Group (UK) Ltd
Croydon, CR0 4YY

CONTENTS

PROLOGUE: HERA'S MEETING

Scene: the palace of Zeus and Hera in Olympia.

Hera: Welcome, you two. Do come in and sit yourselves down. As you know, my dear husband is away visiting the Ethiopians. Now I understand you two have recently had your little differences but I'm hoping that because the war is now over we can work together on a new project.

Aphrodite: Our little differences! Yes, you could say that *(turning towards Athena)*, when the holy city of Troy is a smoking ruin – through your trickery, Athena – and my dear son-in-law, Paris Alexandros, lies dead, shot by an arrow guided by you.

Athena: Correct me if I'm wrong, but wasn't it Paris who started this whole war by kidnapping the wife of a Greek king?

Aphrodite: Helen wasn't kidnapped. She chose to go because she was in love with Paris.

Athena: A love imposed by you. We all know how you operate in such cases, don't we, Hera?

Hera: Could we possibly forget the past for a moment, and turn to the future? I've asked you here this evening as I have an important suggestion to make. I'm sure you both agree that we – and by we I mean both gods and

1

mortals – have just lived through an epic age in our history, an age when mortals and even the gods of Olympus clashed together on the battlefield.

Aphrodite: And an age when our great leader could never make up his mind which side he was on, which made things much worse.

Hera: True enough, but this is not really the topic I wanted to discuss with you. It's important, I think, to try and keep a record of all this history before it completely disappears from memory. Now, we all know the stories about recent events as recited by the bards. Well, do you not feel that these accounts are a little bit biased in that they tend to play down the role of us gods and exaggerate the achievements of mortals – the so-called 'heroes'?

Athena: I agree completely. When the bards sing about the war they hardly mention the part I played in supporting the Greeks, and in protecting their leaders like Achilles and Odysseus from danger, and advising them on what to do next.

Hera: What do you think, Aphrodite?

Aphrodite: I think that when mortals go to war they forget everything except how best to wound and kill. In their bloodlust they ignore why the war started or how it might be brought to a peaceful end. And the bards are just as bad. They don't want to sing about someone like me who just tries her best to save innocent people from death.

Hera: Well, there you are. And this is where I suggest you two come in. My idea is that both of you compose a history of recent events as seen from your own points of view. I'll do the same – in fact I've already started.

Aphrodite: Must we stick to recent events? I mean, if we're

2

telling our own stories why not go right back to our miraculous births, etc.? Do a kind of biography.

Hera: Good point – actually I was just going to say the same thing.

Athena: Then we could get our own versions written down on parchment in this new writing which they use at the court of Mycenae.

Hera: You could, but it so happens that the city-state of Mycenae is about to disappear from the map, and so, unfortunately, will this old-fashioned kind of writing. So nobody would ever be able to read your accounts. No, the best thing to do once you've decided what to say is to go and consult the muses and their mother, Mnemosyne [*Memory*]. You probably know they all live on Mount Helicon in Boeotia. Probably Calliope would be the best one to help. She can explain how to sort out your thoughts in such a way that the bards can recite them at parties – and then they will definitely be remembered.

Aphrodite: We can certainly do that. But if, as you say, Mycenae is about to disappear doesn't this mean that all those parties will cease to be held, and the bards find themselves out of a job?

Hera: No, I don't think it will be as bad as that. And anyway, my knowledge of the future tells me it won't be too long before the Greeks get to know about a completely new kind of writing based on letters, in which your accounts can be written down properly. I can even tell you the name of the author who will start this process. His name is – or rather will be – Homer, and he will be born on the island of Chios.

Athena: How on earth can you go on about sending letters to people before you've even decided what writing to use?

Hera: I don't mean that kind of letter. I mean the alphabet. If you don't understand what I'm talking about then you'll just have to wait and see. Or ask Calliope.

CHAPTER 1: APHRODITE

Where should I start the story Hera has asked me to compose? I'll start with what was perhaps the worst day of my life: the day I was wounded by a mortal. I have a son, Aeneas, who is a fearless Trojan warrior. During the long struggle against the Greek invaders I used to pass my days watching over him from above, wrapped in a dark cloud. Hera and Athena too, my enemies in that war, were never far from the battlefield, and once I heard Athena giving advice to Diomedes, a powerful Greek leader whom she greatly admired and loved.

'You must never try to fight the immortal gods,' she told him. 'Avoid conflict with any of them except Aphrodite – if she enters the fighting you may stab her with the sharp bronze.'

Later I was horrified to see this Diomedes approaching my son, who leapt from his chariot to face him. Diomedes threw his spear at Aeneas who, just in time, ducked from its path. Then he lifted up a huge boulder and swung it at Aeneas. It hit him on the hip, smashing the cup where the thigh bone turns on the hip joint. He dropped to his knees and stayed there. He would certainly have been killed had I not rushed down to pick him up in my arms, intending to remove him from the field of battle, but Diomedes stabbed me in the wrist. From the gash streamed my divine blood, my ichor, and the pain was excruciating, like nothing I had ever suffered before in my whole life. I was forced to let go of my son's body and he was carried to safety by Apollo. I fled in agony up to Olympus, and to Dione, whom I call my darling mother because she has looked after me ever since I first arrived at the home of the gods.

'Save me, Mother, dear. I have been grievously hurt.'

Taking me in her arms she soothed me, asking, 'Which of the gods has wounded you so spitefully, my child? I'm sure you never deserved such punishment.'

Sobbing, I replied, 'It wasn't a god at all but a mortal. Diomedes, he is called. He speared me when I was only trying to save my son. I tell you, mother, this conflict is no longer just between Greeks and Trojans. Those brutal killers, the Greeks, are now at war with the gods themselves.'

'How can this reckless Diomedes be so foolish as to dare attack a god?' my mother asked. 'He will certainly be punished for that. Life isn't long for the man who fights the immortals.'

'Athena told him he could. She said I had no business to be on the battlefield at all and he could attack me whenever he wanted.'

'She was quite wrong to say that. But please don't cry, my darling. Your arm will heal itself, and your pain will soon be over.'

Athena and Hera were watching me and Dione as she wiped away the ichor from my wound, and Athena teased Zeus, who was also watching, with mocking words:

'Oh Father, it's such a shame. Dear Aphrodite was coaxing some young Greek girl to go with the Trojans, and when she was caressing her she scratched her delicate hand on a dress pin.'

Zeus just laughed, and turning to me said, 'War is not for you, my child. You stick to the work of love, and leave the fighting to others.'

Meanwhile Aeneas received divine treatment for his wound from Apollo and his sister, Artemis. He was back on the battlefield the following morning with a new hip joint. You can imagine what I felt about Athena after this event. I never liked her much in the first place but the way she had encouraged Diomedes to stab me made our relationship colder still.

*

I never had a birth mother (nor, come to think of it, a birth father either). I was born from the white foam that arose when Chronos, the father of Zeus, cut off the genitals from his own father, Uranus, with a flint knife, and threw them into the sea. It was from this foam that I emerged near the island of Cythera, and from there I floated on to Cyprus, coming ashore at what is now the city of Paphos. That is why I am often known as Cytherea (*Lady of Cythera*), or Cypris (*Lady of Cyprus*) because both places claim to be where I first came out of the sea.

As soon as I was born I knew what my true nature was, and Zeus came to Paphos and took me up to Olympia to introduce me to the other gods, and to explain my duties. I was then adopted by Zeus and Dione, his consort at the time. Everyone could see that I was the most beautiful goddess of them all, and it was quite appropriate that I was to be the goddess of love and sexual passion. My powers are over everything living – birds and animals, humans and gods. I am like Atlas, who carries the world on his shoulders – since without love and sex the world would soon grind to a halt, would it not?

As you might expect, I myself am passionate. During my life I have made love to many; to gods who seek me out, and occasionally to humans whom I find attractive and who respect me and pray to me. In fact I make little distinction between mortals and immortals when it comes to sex. I am not like those so-called virgin goddesses – Athena and Artemis for example – who would not dream of coupling with a mortal, though they think nothing of brutal punishment for one who gets in their way. It was Athena who changed the peasant girl Arachne into a spider because she challenged her to a weaving competition, and who blinded Tiresias because he stumbled on her bathing naked in the woods. It was most likely Artemis who sent the great boar that killed my young lover Adonis when he was out hunting.

Athena, in particular, has always done her best to challenge or irritate me. I remember one incident soon after I arrived in Olympia. I was exploring the various halls and palaces of the gods and I came across an unusual loom which you could operate sitting down. I had heard that Athena told everyone she had invented it herself. I thought I would try it out but she saw me and went and complained to Zeus. I was given a lecture about how weaving was no concern of mine, and how I should stick to love and its problems. Soon afterwards I retaliated when Athena gave us all a performance on her newly designed flute. As she played she found she had to contort her face in various ways, and I pretended to imitate her, causing the other goddesses to giggle. She was so embarrassed she stopped playing and hurled the flute off the mountain, screaming that the next person to play it would die in agony. I believe it was picked up by a satyr called Marsyas who practised on it and later challenged Apollo to a music contest. He lost the contest and as a result was flayed alive (although Apollo always denied doing the flaying).

I am told that my most divine features are my lovely neck, lush breasts and flashing eyes; plus the fact that I am usually seen laughing or smiling. Due to my incredible beauty I caused a lot of problems on Olympus when I first arrived. Poseidon, Ares, Apollo, Hermes, and even my step-father, Zeus, all wanted me for themselves (by the way, incestuous relationships are permitted among immortals). As a result, Hera, goddess of marriage, decided she would stop any bitter rivalry involving the Olympic family by picking a husband for me. She chose her son, Hephaestus, who was rather ugly by our standards, and had a pronounced limp. She reckoned no one could ever be jealous of him. He was over-joyed with Hera's offer, and we were married by Zeus.

I suppose Hephaestus has, by and large, turned out to be a thoughtful and loving husband to me. He is a highly skilled craftsman, especially concerning anything to do with metal. His workshop and forge are on Olympia, though some way distant from our living halls so we won't be polluted by smoke. He has a team of experienced assistants who are mostly Cyclopes, those giant one-eyed creatures, and between them they can produce anything we gods ask for. Such requests have included: thunderbolts for Zeus, a winged helmet and sandals for Hermes, a bow and arrows for our son Eros. Did I mention I gave birth to a son early in our marriage? Eros is a mischievous little boy but he usually does what I tell him, and the magic arrows made for him by his father have solved many erotic issues.

During our marriage Hephaestus has given me lots of lovely presents made by him, though easily the most important was his wedding present to me: a leather girdle. It fits under my breasts, pushing them forward, and then goes down to between my legs, fastening at the back. It's a magic girdle. When I have it on, the person I am talking to is instantly attracted to me – assuming they weren't already!

I must admit that I have not always been faithful to this loving husband of mine – hardly surprising since I am the goddess of love and sex. This brings me to that famous incident about the net, which was the one occasion when Hephaestus tried to humiliate and embarrass me. At the time, I was having an affair with Ares, god of war – rather unexpected perhaps considering that, unlike me, he is obsessed with the brutality and carnage of battle. However, he is also young, muscular and good-looking. It seems my husband had been told of our relationship, and one day he pretended he had to make a trip to Lesbos. He had secretly designed an unbreakable golden net which fell down on us from the ceiling as soon as we jumped naked into bed together. The more we struggled the tighter we were caught in the net. Hephaestus then appeared, and invited the other gods to come and view us, whereupon there was much laughter, with Athena taking the lead in jeering at me. It was only after a large ransom had been agreed between Ares and Hephaestus that we were released.

As I said, I have had many lovers, gods and mortals, men and women. But there have been very few whom I have truly loved. One of these was Adonis, a beautiful and slightly effeminate young prince who died at far too young an age. I will briefly recount the story of his birth – which, by the way, reflects little credit on me. His mother was

Myrrha, a princess from Paphos, whose own mother used to brag that her daughter was more beautiful than me. I am afraid that, like all gods, I am highly conscious of my status, so when I heard this I cursed poor Myrrha with an insatiable love for her father, Cinyras, who was the King of Paphos. Cinyras, when drunk one evening, was informed that a certain young girl had knocked on the palace door announcing that she was in love with him and wanted to sleep with him. This of course was Myrrha, and for several nights she visited him when it was dark and they made love. When he finally realised he had been tricked into sex with his own daughter he rushed after her with a drawn sword aiming to kill her. Escaping from him, Myrrha wandered in exile for months, afraid of death, tired of life, and pregnant. She begged the gods for help, and was transformed into the myrrh tree (later named after her), but I managed to save the newly born Adonis from inside the tree. I handed him over to Persephone, goddess of the underworld, to bring him up. But she was so enchanted by his beauty that when he was older she refused to return him to me. I asked Zeus to judge between us and he allowed Persephone to keep him for four months each year, me to have him for another four months, and the rest of the year Adonis himself could choose. He chose me and we became lovers. We spent many idyllic months together, but one day when he was out hunting he met a fierce boar which gored him to death. I still don't know for certain who sent the boar. Possibly Artemis, or perhaps Ares because he was jealous of my relationship with Adonis.

As an immortal I find it difficult to construct a reliable narrative of my life, or to say what events took place and when – so please don't expect precise dates from me! For mortals, of course, time is really important when you know you only have a limited amount of it; old age and death are always just round the corner. But for us past and future stretch out interminably, and the only significant moment is the present. Anyway, this is my excuse if I sometimes confuse events or get them in the wrong order. So, for instance, I may be wrong when I say that it was soon after the net incident that Zeus decided to send me off to seduce a mortal. He chose to frame it as a semi-humorous challenge: 'See if you can make love to this handsome young stranger.' Possibly he was hoping I might leave the gods alone, at least for a time. Perhaps he thought he was punishing me, though actually I enjoyed the experience, and didn't view it as a punishment at all. The mortal Zeus chose for me was Anchises, a young cowherd who lived a fairly lonely life on the slopes of Mount Ida, not far from the city of Troy. In fact, although temporarily working on a farm, Anchises was of noble blood. He was also distantly related to Priam, King of Troy.

To seduce Anchises I first went to my sanctuary at Paphos to bathe and dress, and there the Graces washed me and anointed me with ambrosial oil, our favourite ointment. So as not to frighten him I decided to take on the appearance of a beautiful young human girl. I wore bright clothing and gleaming jewels, and underneath, of course, my magic girdle. Then I went in search of Anchises whom I found resting outside his hut after his day's work in the fields. He was impressed by my looks and asked whether I was a goddess, or perhaps one of the nymphs that lived on this mountain. I told him no, I was mortal, a girl from a royal family. I said my father was the King of Phrygia, a country far to the east. He then asked how, in that case, I had found my way to Mount Ida, so I made up a story to suit my appearance. I explained I had been at home that morning in my father's gardens, dancing with a crowd of other girls in honour of Artemis when suddenly Hermes, winged messenger of the gods, had descended from the sky and spirited me away. Hermes told me I had been picked by Zeus to be the bride of the Trojan prince, Anchises, and mother of his children. He transported me across mountains and rivers to this spot where we now were. There was a pause while Anchises tried to collect his thoughts. Then he asked, suspiciously, how it was that I, a Phrygian maiden, spoke the Trojan language so fluently, and I explained that when I was a little girl I had been looked after by a Trojan nurse.

I saw that while we talked Anchises was struck by intense sexual longing for me.

'If you are truly to be my wife,' he said, 'then no one can stop me from making love to you this very evening.'

As befitted an innocent young girl I cast my eyes down and pretended to hesitate but he took me by the hand and led me into his little cottage. Hung all around the bedroom were the skins of bears and lions he had killed on the mountain when protecting his sheep. Stripping off our clothes, we climbed onto his bed.

After we had made passionate love I stood up and reverted to my real appearance as a goddess – tall and radiant. Anchises was terrified because he had heard stories about how mortals who slept with gods were punished.

'Don't be afraid,' I told him. 'So long as you keep our lovemaking secret no harm will come to you.'

Then I explained the plan.

'In due course I shall bear you a son, to be named Aeneas, and he will always receive my protection. But for the first years of his life this child is to be brought up by the nymphs of Mount Ida, until the time comes to hand him

13

over to you, his father.'

On this we parted, I to return to Olympus. Later I heard that Anchises had boasted to his friends that he had made love to the goddess Aphrodite. Zeus was angry and had struck him on the leg with a thunderbolt, which made him limp for the rest of his life. I never saw Anchises again, but his son Aeneas did receive my full protection, as I shall shortly relate.

We gods much enjoy picking out particular mortals whose qualities we admire and who have been particularly loyal to us. Then we try and help them as much as we can. In my case I should like to mention two: Theseus, who was the son of the King of Athens, and Helen of Sparta. When I first came to know Theseus he had just volunteered to be among the fourteen young men and women that Athens was pledged to send to Crete every nine years to be sacrificed to the Minotaur. This was a ferocious monster, half-man and half-bull, whom Minos, the ruler of Crete, kept in a specially built labyrinth. Young Theseus hoped to become famous as the hero who had killed the Minotaur, though he had little idea how to achieve this and then escape from the labyrinth. I caused Ariadne, daughter of Minos, to fall in love with him and help him. She gave him a ball of thread which he was able to attach to the gate when he entered the labyrinth and unwind as he searched for the Minotaur. He found the creature fast asleep and managed to strangle it with his bare hands. Then he followed the thread back to the gate he came in by, and escaped with the other young Athenians, taking Ariadne with him.

On the way back to Athens there was a powerful storm. Ariadne became very ill and Theseus put her ashore on the island of Naxos to recover while repairs were done to his ship. But violent winds carried them far out to sea, and by the time they got back to Naxos they found that Ariadne had disappeared. Later I was told that a young demi-god named Dionysus had taken her from the island and made her his wife.

Since then I have followed Theseus's many adventures, and have helped him whenever I could. In due course, Theseus inherited the throne of Athens from his father. He built a temple dedicated to me on the Acropolis, although he also worshipped my rival, Athena, patron goddess of Athens. Theseus was a wise and popular ruler, but his love life was less successful. He had several wives in succession, none of whom survived very long. Then for a time he was single. You can imagine my surprise therefore when one day, while I was walking the streets of the city disguised as a mortal, I came across him arm in arm with a young girl whom I knew well.

This was Helen of Sparta, and I had followed her ever since her extraordinary conception, some fifteen years earlier. Her mother, Leda, had been married to the King of Sparta, Tyndareus, but before that she had been a priestess of the Great Goddess whose worship, popular among women, preceded that of the Olympian gods and goddesses. In Sparta they used to hold a dramatic ceremony every year in a remote wooded glade, with Leda as the chief priestess representing the Goddess. She had to lie naked on a plinth surrounded by worshippers to receive a facsimile of her bird-consort representing the natural world – so I've been told; don't ask me how it worked. But one year it was said that Zeus, looking down from Olympus, observed the ceremony, and was so taken by Leda's loveliness that he swooped down in the shape of a giant swan and made love to her. The result was Helen. Of course Tyndareus soon heard what had happened, and in his anger he called Leda

15

a faithless whore, and from then on did his best to wipe out all traces of this old religion in Sparta. And as Helen grew up it became obvious to everyone that she couldn't possibly be the daughter of Tyndareus. He was narrow-faced, swarthy, with a nose like the beak of a hawk, whereas she was white, with prominent cheekbones and a mass of red-gold hair. He used to lose his temper and start shouting at mother and daughter, and when I visited them I often saw Leda sitting alone in her bedroom, her eyes red from crying.

I was worried that Hera would take revenge on this innocent girl merely because Zeus was her father – as she had done to so many other children who were the result of her husband's numerous affairs. However, she did nothing – possibly she never even knew about the mating of the giant swan, though that seems unlikely.

Helen had a miserable childhood. Her father hated her because people knew she was not his daughter, which was a source of laughter and scorn throughout the kingdom. He much preferred her elder sister, Clytemnestra, and her two younger brothers, Castor and Pollux. Clytemnestra, who looked more like Tyndareus (though much prettier), was four years older than Helen. She was jealous of her sister's beauty, and she and her friends teased and bullied her as much as they could. Tyndareus was also unkind and often brutal to his own wife. The cruellest day in Helen's young life came when she was only five and was informed by a servant that her mother had gone to the sacred grove where once she had worshipped the Great Goddess, and there had hung herself from the branch of an oak tree, leaving her four young children without a mother.

There came the time when Clytemnestra was to be married. The husband Tyndareus chose for her was the most powerful man in all Greece, Agamemnon, King of Mycenae. Of course everyone knew about Agamemnon: his subjects treated him almost like a god, his wealth exceeded every other king, his ships dominated every coast. Obviously, this was to be a political marriage – Tyndareus was excited by the possibility of an alliance between Sparta and Mycenae. I should add that I intensely disliked Agamemnon, even though his worst crime was still to come. Already he had managed to offend myself and other gods by his ruthless desecration of our temples in search of anything made of bronze which could be melted down and used for making weapons. He was a man much more interested in making war than making love. But Clytemnestra herself was excited by the prospect of becoming Queen of Mycenae. It was a relief to Helen when the time came for her sister to marry and leave home.

And this seems to be a suitable moment to end this, the first – rather too long – instalment of my personal story.

CHAPTER 2: ATHENA

My mother is Metis, the first wife of Zeus. She was a Titan, one of the gods who once ruled the world, but who had been overthrown by the Olympians. When Metis was first pregnant with me, Zeus was given a prophecy that she would bear him a child who would overthrow him just as he had once overthrown his own father, Chronos. So he challenged her to a shape-shifting competition, and when she changed into a fly he swallowed her. But I lived on inside Metis and grew stronger. I learnt to hear my mother's thoughts, even though we were both imprisoned in the brain of Zeus. One day she told me:

'I am leaving you now, but I have bequeathed you all my powers. Soon you will be able to break out from Zeus and start your new life. I give you a spear which will help you do this, and which will defend you against future enemies. Be cautious when you first speak to Zeus. Do not mention my name, say only that he is your father. Goodbye, my darling child.'

With that, Metis vanished and I was left in the dark prison of Zeus's head. I started to stab repeatedly with my new spear against the walls of my prison until a thin line of light appeared and I tore at the gash with my hands to widen it. When the hole was large enough I climbed out, spear and all. As I got to my feet I felt my body expand. In front of me was a huge figure, dressed in the purple robes of a king, with solid gold armbands covering his biceps. His long hair and thick beard were both a deep black. Ichor was flowing from a wound in his head, and with both hands he was trying to press together the edges of the gash. In a few moments it ceased to flow and the wound healed itself. Noticing that Zeus was now looking at me with astonishment and extreme distrust, I hastened to pacify him, remembering my mother's instructions. In my newly acquired voice I cried out:

'Hail, almighty Zeus. I am your daughter, Athena, goddess of wisdom and war. Born from your brain, and without a mother, I look to you alone for guidance and instruction in this world.'

Laying my spear down, I knelt in front of him and added, 'My life is at your command and I will always follow your will.'

After he had recovered from his shock at my sudden appearance, Zeus handed me over to his new wife Hera to be looked after. Hera was clearly sceptical about what I had said about my birth:

'My husband claims you were born from his head, and not of any goddess or mortal mother. Can this be true?'

I hastened to reassure her, but it was obvious that her suspicions were never fully satisfied. There would always be this barrier to any close relationship between Hera and me. However, Hera did put her young sister Hestia in charge of my upbringing. As a young goddess I already had the powers and skills inherited from my mother, and I really just needed to practise them. I did enjoy transforming myself into different people. When meeting another god you don't need to change yourself, but when we gods meet a mortal we often alter our appearance and pretend to be another mortal, perhaps someone that person knows. This is because if we appear as we really are – tall, beautiful, radiant – the mortal we are talking to is often so overcome that they can't think or speak clearly. In the case of Zeus, seeing him as he really was could actually be fatal. I think it was one of his lovers, Semele, who made him promise to reveal to her his true shape, and when he did she was burnt to death by the fiery rays shining from his body!

The kind of things Hestia helped me with were: invisibility, travelling through the air, smoothing the sea or creating winds, etc. Also, during the peaceful mornings spent in Zeus's palace I was introduced to the usual feminine arts such as singing, and also spinning and weaving.

When not working with Hestia I was looked after by the palace slaves who did the cooking and cleaning, heated water for baths, and told me stories about the other gods and goddesses. It was an idyllic existence, and I was free to wander round Olympia as much as I liked. One day I heard the banging of a hammer, and on investigation saw through an open door the glow of a furnace. It turned out to be the workshop of Hephaestus, the god of fire, metal-working and sculpture. I had been told about Hephaestus, who was lame, and not particularly handsome. He was one of the sons of Zeus and Hera. The palace servants had whispered to me that Zeus had made him marry the beautiful Aphrodite so as to stop quarrels between other gods fighting for her hand. I went down, knocked on the door and introduced myself.

'Welcome, Athena,' he said. ' I am just making a sword for Ares. Would you like to watch? That is, if you can stand the heat in here.'

Hephaestus opened a wooden mould into which he had earlier poured liquid bronze. He took out the hardened metal which then needed to be hammered and heated repeatedly until it started looking like a sword. Finally, it was taken outside for sharpening.

'Here, have a go,' he offered. 'Don't sharpen it too much. Remember it's only a practice sword.'

He showed me how to hold it to the grindstone while he went to look for a suitable hilt and sheath. When the sword was ready he handed it to me.

'This can be for you,' he said. 'After all, you did help make it. It's a bit rough and ready but you might find it useful, and I can easily make another one for Ares.'

I was delighted, and from now on this was my sword whenever I could find someone to practise with.

As I grew older I began to realise I did not fit comfortably into the usual categories of male or female. Of course I knew I was physically a girl, which was why I had told Zeus I was his daughter, but in my mind I often felt I was neither the one thing nor the other. To start with, I couldn't bear the thought that one day I should have to marry and make love to someone. In fact I swore an oath to myself that I would never do such a thing, even if Zeus ordered me to.

Then again, I was fascinated by anything to do with war and violence. I often appeared in public wearing a bronze breastplate and helmet and carrying the spear my mother had given me. On the other hand, I also became very interested in certain domestic pursuits, such as making cloth, and preparing food. I have invented several things to make the labours of mortal women easier, such as fired clay pots for cooking and storage, and a horizontal loom that one can operate sitting down.

When Hestia had taught me all she knew, Zeus decided that I needed some earthly experience to mature me, so he sent me down to live at the home of the river god Triton and his five daughters. This was again a happy time for me, though it did not end happily. I shared a cottage beside the river with the five water nymphs, and we were free all day to run around after each other, ride horses or swim in the river. My best friend was Pallas, the oldest sister, and we became quite intimate. We used to go for long walks together, or practise our skills with bows and arrows, or spears and swords. Sometimes we were visited by other gods from Olympus, and one fairly frequent visitor was my young half-brother Ares, the god of war, who gave us tips on how to fight. It soon became clear to everyone that the reason Ares appeared so often was because he had fallen for Pallas, and finally she admitted to me that she and Ares didn't just practise armed combat, but also kissing when no one else was around.

'You must agree he is terribly handsome, even for a god,' she whispered. 'And he's a wonderful kisser. But he never tries to go any further than that.'

Pallas and I thought we were becoming pretty good at sword fighting, what with advice from Ares and our own skills. I was probably the stronger one, but Pallas was very quick moving. It seemed that news of our progress had reached Olympia because one day a message reached us that Zeus would like to come and see for himself. This was especially pleasing to me because I hadn't seen him for months and had begun to think he had forgotten all about me. So a week later, there was Zeus - seated on a special throne by the river, and surrounded by several other gods including Hera, Hestia and Ares, together with Pallas's whole family and their servants.

After the lavish picnic which Triton laid on had been cleared away, Pallas and I took up our practice swords and light leather shields. With a wave of Zeus' hand, we started to circle round each other looking for an opening. Pallas went on the attack first with a series of rapid thrusts, each of which I managed to parry. We were fighting at our best, no doubt because of the audience. When Pallas made an especially ambitious thrust which briefly unbalanced her, I saw my chance and lifted my sword high for an overhead blow. Pallas saw it coming and was just about to block it with her shield when Zeus suddenly rose from his throne and in a piercing voice bellowed, 'STOP!' but it was too late. My sword came down with all my force behind it, and Pallas froze before her shield was in position to block the blow. The sword struck her long, delicate neck causing blood to spurt from the wound. I dropped my blood-stained sword and ran to help her but there was nothing I could do. She collapsed onto the grass, and in a few seconds her life had ebbed away. Everyone was screaming and shouting though Zeus remained standing and said nothing. I ran up to him.

'Father, save her,' I begged, but he shook his head.

'My child, it is too late. Her spirit is already on its way to the underworld. It is not your fault.'

'Then I shall go down to Hades and beg him to let her come back to us,' I said.

'I don't think that will be allowed,' was the reply.

But I did go.

From Hestia and others I had been told something about the underworld, the realm of the dead, but I had never met Hades, Zeus's brother, who was its king. I shimmered eastwards across land and sea, and arrived at the entrance to the underworld, which was close to the great river

23

Oceanus that encircles the world. Cerberus, the huge three-headed hound that guards the gates, recognised me as an immortal, and let me pass with a respectful nod of one of his heads. After I had wandered round for some time I met an official who took me to meet my uncle Hades. I was surprised to see how tall and elegant he was, very unlike my stocky, bearded father. I explained about the terrible accident and how guilty I felt about what had happened. Could my friend possibly be released back to the land of the living?

'Dear Athena, I am so very sorry,' he replied. 'We get many requests like yours but rules are rules, and once the spirit has entered the underworld it can never return. As an immortal you will see many mortals die. That's why it's always wise not to get too close.'

I begged Hades at least to be allowed to speak to Pallas but at first he was not keen for me to do even that.

'Uncle,' I pleaded, 'she was my best friend. I'm sure she would at least want to see me one more time.'

Hades finally agreed somewhat reluctantly and together we transported ourselves to the bank of a river where a group of nymphs, among them Pallas, were laughing and splashing water at each other. I noticed the wound in Pallas's neck seemed to have healed. Hades called her over to where we were standing. He put his finger on her forehead, and she gasped as memories came flooding back into her mind.

'Pallas,' I cried as I hugged her. 'I'm so sorry. I never meant to hurt you.'

'Athena,' she replied, 'what are you doing here? I know you didn't mean to hurt me.' Then she whispered, 'It was Zeus. He wanted to kill me because Ares loved me. He didn't want his son to marry a mere water nymph. By shouting stop, he threw me off just enough for you to kill me – just as planned.'

'How can you ever forgive me?' I sobbed.

'I can forgive you because it wasn't your fault. But I have to say goodbye now.'

Turning to Hades, she asked him to once more erase all memories of her previous life. He gave her a sip from a small bottle of water he had in his pocket, taken from the river Styx, and it was done. When Pallas looked at me again there was no recognition in her eyes. Hades signed for her to go back to her friends. All that remained for me was to thank him for his help, and retrace my steps back to the gates of the underworld, and then to Olympus. I felt sure that Triton and his family would always blame me for Pallas's death. My life with them had come to an end.

My confidence as a goddess steadily increased, but still I was aware that I was not as powerful as I could be. Like all gods, I needed the support and worship of mortals – their prayers, their sacrifices, their temples – in order to invigorate myself. Most of the other immortals already had clear roles on earth, and temples dedicated to them. Then one day it was announced that the inhabitants of Attica, a relatively prosperous region of Greece close to the sea, had petitioned Zeus to find them a suitable god to be their patron. The population of Attica was on the increase, and their king, Cecrops, felt that the little town where he had just built himself a palace had the potential, with divine favour, to become a leading Greek port.

Zeus held a meeting in Olympia to discuss this petition and see if there were any volunteers to become Attica's patron. At the meeting, Zeus's other brother Poseidon spoke up, explaining that if it was a question of developing a new port he, as god of the seas, was the obvious choice.

He was the only god who could help guard the crews of trading ships from Attica in their journeys across the world. No other god seemed interested in challenging Poseidon until I stood up, surprising the others.

'I know I am relatively inexperienced,' I said, 'however, I believe I have already made some contribution to human happiness and prosperity. I believe I am the ideal choice to take on this new role.'

Poseidon's irritation when I said this was palpable, but Zeus was clearly pleased that his youngest daughter was showing some ambition. He agreed to a suggestion from the meeting that the people of Attica and their king should be invited to make the final choice between us. It was decided the two candidates should each present a gift to Attica, and then it would be up to the people as to whom to choose.

The following week Poseidon and I arrived at the top of a rocky hill that looked down on the new town where Cecrops had built his palace. A crowd of men and women, most of them local farmers, were waiting for us, and we were greeted by the king and his counsellors. Poseidon spoke first. He explained that, unlike his young niece, he was one of the most experienced and powerful gods of Olympus. Also, as god of the sea and the winds he would of course be able to protect from danger all those who set out from, or visited, their new port.

'And here is my gift to your precious land,' he shouted, as he stabbed hard with his trident into the dry, stony earth. Immediately, water gushed out from the hole he had made, forming a stream that flowed down the hill. There were gasps of surprise followed by applause from the crowd. King Cecrops looked delighted.

'Oh thank you, Lord Poseidon. The greatest problem

faced by the farmers of Attica is how to irrigate their fields, and clearly your gift will be of immense help to us.'

He bent down to taste a handful of the water, and his expression suddenly changed.

'But this water tastes of salt!' he cried out as he turned to face his people.

'Well of course it does,' replied Poseidon. 'After all, I am the lord of the seas.'

I smiled to myself as I realised that my rival was either exceedingly stupid or totally ignorant of agriculture – or both.

It was now the moment for me to announce my gift to the people of Attica. From my pocket I produced a tiny seed and a bottle of (fresh) water. Choosing a spot some way from Poseidon's stream, I dug a small hole, placed my seed in it, covered the hole with earth and watered it thoroughly. Then, putting my hand palm downwards just above the wet earth, I willed the seed to sprout. Within a few minutes a plant emerged, and quickly grew into a full-sized tree bearing flowers, followed by clusters of small purple fruits. I turned to the crowd.

'I name this tree the olive tree. It is ideal for your land and climate, and will last for hundreds of years through hot summers and icy winters. Its fruits are rich in useful oils and I think you will find them tasteful. I invite all of you to try them. Oh and please keep the stones for replanting!'

All the farmers and their wives surged forward to taste the olives, and there were animated discussions and cries of satisfaction.

King Cecrops then led Poseidon and me to a nearby tent where we were invited to sample the local wine, while he and his people debated their verdict. It was not long before the king reappeared, to announce that the verdict had been unanimous. He invited me to be the divine patron of Attica, an honour I accepted with gratitude, promising always to support the interests of the Attican people. Everyone went down on their knees and I suddenly felt a surge of raw energy which made me stagger back. When I recovered I felt stronger than I had ever been. I gasped in delight. So this was what it felt like – the power that flowed to a god from human worship. Sometime later I heard that the people of Attica wanted to call their new city 'Athens' in my honour.

It only remains to say that Poseidon, feeling humiliated by losing the contest, never completely forgave me, and relations between the two of us have remained tense ever since. But Zeus told me he was proud of my achievement. I'm pretty certain in fact that I am his favourite among all the goddesses. Hera is still not so sure about me, even though we did collaborate during the war that was to come. Still, I must admit I do admire Hera for always standing up to her philandering husband, and never being afraid of him even though he could so easily punish her, or even demolish her completely with a thunderbolt.

During my time as an Olympic goddess I have been credited with inventing a vast array of useful things to help mortals. For example, as well as the pots and the loom I mentioned before, it is often claimed that I was the one who first taught the science of numbers, as well as contributing to all women's pursuits, including cooking, weaving, and spinning. Not to mention the plough, the rake, the ox-yoke, the horse-bridle, the chariot and even the ship. Not all these attributions are actually true, but because the other gods rarely come up with anything original or useful, such inventions are often put down to me.

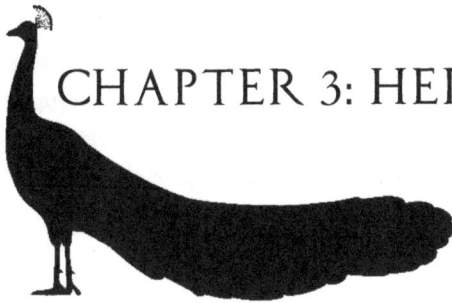

CHAPTER 3: HERA

I am a daughter of the Titans, Chronos and Rhea, which makes me the sister of Zeus. But I also married Zeus, becoming second only to my husband in power. Together with him I rule the gods of Olympus. I am also personally the goddess of mortal women, of marriage, and of the family. I am worshipped all over the world. My earliest temple was on the island of Samos, but there are now temples dedicated to me throughout Greece. Before the Trojan war began I was particularly honoured in Sparta and Mycenae, where the brothers Menelaus and Agamemnon were the kings, as well as in Argos, the kingdom of another Greek hero, Diomedes, whom I much admired. No wonder I supported the Greek side in that lengthy war.

As to my birth, it was unusual, not to say magical (as also, I suppose, were the births of both Athena and Aphrodite). I was in a sense born twice, as I shall explain. My father, Chronos, had castrated his own father, Uranus, and then imprisoned him deep into the earth, but before he was locked away Uranus had time to warn Chronos that one day his own son would do the same to him. Consequently, when Chronos and his wife, Rhea, started having children, he took care to seize each baby as soon as it was born, and swallow it. Rhea was powerless. I was the fifth child to be treated in this fashion, and by this time Rhea's love for Chronos had evaporated, and turned into bitter hatred. So before the birth, she prepared a potion that contained an emetic to force Chronos to vomit, together with poppy juice to make him sleep. Then she found a suitable stone and wrapped it in swaddling clothes. Chronos drank the potion and unknowingly swallowed the stone thinking it was a baby. The emetic worked like a charm, and Chronos spewed up the stone and also the five little children he had once swallowed. Then he fell into a deep sleep while we children laughed at our new freedom, and danced with our mother who had meanwhile given birth to Zeus. And the five of us swore allegiance to Zeus, our new king, who had helped free us from the prison of Chronos's stomach.

From my earliest days Zeus was attracted to me, but Rhea warned me not to make love to him unless he promised to marry me. One day he disguised himself as a bedraggled cuckoo and when I took pity on him and held him close between my breasts he suddenly resumed his true shape and forced himself on me. After that he did promise to marry me, and preparations for a great wedding were discussed. At about the same time Zeus chose Olympus, Greece's highest mountain, as our future home. I was at the peak of happiness. Not only was I to marry Zeus and become the queen of the Olympian gods but also I was pregnant and fully expected my future child would possess all the qualities necessary to one day succeed his father as King of Olympus.

To my dismay the baby turned out to be not only unnaturally small, like a tiny doll, but also dark, swarthy and ugly. After one horrified glance I snatched him up and threw him down the mountainside and into the sea far below. I imagined this would be the sad end of Hephaestus – the name I had given him before he was born – and it was not long before I became pregnant again. I had no idea that he had been rescued by the sea-goddess, Thetis, who was to enter more than once into the story of my life. Thetis lived in the sea near Lemnos, and it was on this island that she looked after Hephaestus, watching over his rapid development into childhood and then adolescence. It turned out that he was obsessed with the forging of metals, and possessed special powers when it came to the fashioning of complex and even magical objects, so Thetis provided him with a smithy and co-workers with whom he could practise his skills.

Meanwhile a date had been set for my wedding; invitations were sent out and gifts started to pour in. One present, from an unknown sender, was a handsome golden chair which took my fancy, but when I sat on it to try it out, its arms moved inward to hold me in a tight grip. None of the gods, not even Zeus, could unlock the chair, and I realised that the wedding would have to be postponed or I would become a laughingstock. Zeus proclaimed that whoever could free me might marry the beautiful Aphrodite as a reward. Then an ugly little creature appeared announcing that he was my son, and might possibly be able to help me. As soon as he touched the chair, the arms swung open and I was free. This was of course Hephaestus, whom we now invited to return to Olympus where he was given his own workshop. And when Zeus and I were married, vowing always to be faithful to one another, a second marriage was also celebrated – that of Hephaestus and Aphrodite. Since then I have held to the promise I made at my marriage never to take another lover. Zeus has proved to be an amorous husband, and I have since had three more children by him, the eldest being Ares, the violent and rather unpopular god of war. I may say that I have long since forgiven Hephaestus, my first-born, for his cruel gift, and I have come to appreciate his skills and the work he has done both for me and for the other Olympians.

Unfortunately, from early on in our marriage, Zeus proved himself unable to control his sexual desires. I cannot count the number of times he has seduced either a beautiful nymph or a mortal girl, whether princess or commoner. Sometimes he acts upon impulse like with poor Leda, whom he tricked and raped.

At other times Zeus plans his various affairs, as with the sad story of Princess Semele, the daughter of King Cadmus of Thebes. He had a secret love affair with Semele lasting several months. He first met this young princess when he saw her emerging after a swim in the river near her home. He assumed the guise of a handsome young mortal but then told her who he was, and the two of them made love on the riverbank. They arranged to meet regularly – once a month in fact, when the moon was full. She was six months pregnant before I found out. Zeus was so keen on Semele that at this point he said that when they next met he would give her whatever she asked for, and he backed up this offer by swearing an oath on the river Styx which flowed through the underworld. It was a binding oath which even Zeus himself could not disobey. But I was told all about the affair and about Zeus's promise. I came down to Thebes to visit Semele, disguised as an elderly neighbour of hers, and I advised the princess that she should demand to see her lover in his real nature and form. Otherwise, how could she be sure he was not some kind of evil monster? Now Zeus knew that no mortal could see him as the lord of thunder and lightning and not be consumed by fire, but when she told him what she wanted he could not break his oath. Semele was burnt to death. Naturally I was sorry for this young girl, especially as it was indirectly my fault. However, Hermes, Zeus's servant, was able to snatch her seven-month-old son from her womb and insert it into Zeus's thigh, where the baby matured until it was time for its birth.

This son was named Dionysus, and he was, to my chagrin, to become one of the most popular gods in our Olympic pantheon. When he was young he was said to be exceptionally good looking, even for a demi-god, and he travelled widely. His gift to mankind was the culture of the vine, which he introduced across the known world.

As everyone knows, the drinking of wine has two aspects: it invigorates the mind, allowing men and women to achieve things they might otherwise never have considered, but it also disturbs and confuses so that drinkers may perpetrate ruthless and cruel acts foreign to their normal selves. In other words, a most unnatural beverage.

During its early days, the cult of Dionysus – or Bacchus, his other name – was taken up exclusively by women. These 'Bacchantes' used to leave their homes to wander where the spirit took them, dancing, singing and drinking wine, swept up in a fierce ecstasy. Their leader was a new kind of god who affected the minds of his worshippers, as opposed to gods who merely received prayers and sacrifices. No wonder then that I, Queen of the gods, thoroughly disapproved of this new cult, though I could do little to stop it. I was also not very pleased that Dionysus, who was after all half mortal, was invited to live in with the real immortals. He then went down to Hades to save his mother Semele from death, and brought her back up to Olympia to join us. She was only a human, yet, there was nothing to be done in the face of Zeus's consent.

I myself have never tasted a drop of Dionysus's famous wine, and have no intention of ever doing so.

Occasionally, so as to avoid my notice, my husband transforms a new mistress into a different shape. This happened in the case of the nymph Io, daughter of a river god. One day I happened to notice a lone thundercloud which seemed to be hurrying across an otherwise blue sky. I immediately guessed that this was Zeus, probably up to no good. I rushed down to confront him but he saw me coming and had time to change his mistress into a beautiful little snow-white cow.

I asked him what he was doing, and he said that he had only just noticed this cow and had stopped to admire it while on his travels. Obviously I did not believe a word of it. So I shrewdly said I thought the cow was very pretty, and would he please make me a present of it, and he realised he could hardly refuse without making me suspicious.

I took the cow and tied her to a tree, then sent for my servant Argus Panoptes [*the all-seeing*], who had a hundred eyes, to watch over her. It was never possible to get past Argus since he rarely closed more than half his eyes at once, even at night. But Zeus ordered Hermes to find a way to kill him. Hermes transformed himself into a young shepherd and descended to where Argus was keeping watch. With his reed pipe he played so entrancingly that Argus invited him to sit beside him on his bench. Then Hermes switched to telling stories – stories that were so long and boring that gradually Argus's eyes started to close until finally he fell into a deep sleep, at which point Hermes leapt up, stabbed him to death, and untied Io. I, of course was even more angry when I heard what had happened to my faithful servant.

The little white cow did not escape punishment. I sent a magic gadfly which continuously stung her as she wandered the earth, allowing her little time to sleep, or even to eat and drink. Her miserable journey took her along the shores of the Ionian Sea – later named after her – then across the Bosphorus [*cow passage* – also named after her] and southwards to Egypt. By this time Zeus and I had managed to come to an agreement regarding her fate. Io was transformed back into a human on the understanding that Zeus never look at her again. For the rest of her life she lived in Egypt, founding the new cult of Isis, a goddess who was often portrayed wearing a sun disk between the horns of a cow.

Leda, Semele and Io are just three of my husband's numerous 'seductions.' He may, of course, attempt to have sex with whatever female he takes a fancy to, and I do not have the power to stop him. I just have to use what skills I do possess in order to make things difficult for him and to hope that each of his affairs will be the last. I do feel sorry for the many young girls seduced by my husband, and also guilty about how I have treated many of them, but so often I am simply powerless to help them, in the face of my husband.

During all the time that I was struggling to bring a stop to Zeus's extra-marital love life, all the other gods, including myself, were becoming more and more irritated at his conceit and his oppressive leadership. He was turning into a dictator who never consulted other people's opinions about what to do next. Eventually the time came when we decided to act, and get rid of him as our leader. When he was fast asleep we held him and tied him down with rawhide thongs knotted into a hundred knots so that he could not move a muscle. He threatened us with instant death but we had put his lethal thunderbolts out of reach, and merely laughed at him. Finally it was Thetis, the sea-goddess, who got him untied. She used the hundred-handed giant Briareus, a son of Gaia, to untie all the knots at once. When freed, Zeus decided to punish me as leader of the revolt. He hung me up from the sky with bracelets on each wrist and anvils fastened to my ankles. I was only released when the other gods all swore an oath never to rebel against him again.

My husband's infidelities did not cease.

I admit I can be pretty ruthless when it comes to punishing my husband's lovers and also the children that result from his affairs. People say I never forget or forgive an injury to myself, and when it concerns Zeus's seductions this might well be true (though in the case of Io, I did eventually forgive). But I appeal to the reader of this, my little biography. Can you imagine what it's like to be the goddess of marriages while all the world knows that in your own marriage your husband is constantly cheating on you?

*

Once I decide to support a particular mortal I stick at the task and do my best for them. Here I might compare myself with my colleagues Athena and Aphrodite, the only difference being that their heroes are still alive whereas the most famous of mine has long since died. The young mortal whom I decided to support was Jason, the son of Aeson, King of Iolcus in Thessaly. Jason had a wicked uncle, Pelias, who killed Aeson and made himself king. At this time Jason's mother was about to give birth to him, and she thought Pelias might also kill the baby if she did not send him away to be brought up abroad. When he was eighteen Jason decided to return to Iolcus to check out the situation there and see what chance there was of reclaiming his heritage from his uncle. He soon found out that Pelius was a really unpopular ruler. Jason thought he would visit the annual festival in Iolcus, perhaps to confront Pelias. To do this he had to cross a small river, and sitting on the bank there was a little old woman obviously hoping someone would help her across. This was me. I had come to Iolcus because Pelius had insulted me by desecrating my temple, and I was hoping Jason might help me get rid of him.

While crossing the river with me on his back Jason lost one of his sandals in the mud. He met Pelius who was particularly worried because he had been told by an oracle that a man with only one sandal would succeed him as king of Iolcus, so he hastily thought of a plan to get rid of Jason. He sent him to bring back the Golden Fleece, a precious object with magic healing properties. Jason, with my help, collected a crew that included many of the most famous warriors of the day including Orpheus, Theseus, and Hercules (who quitted the expedition halfway through). They all set out from Thessaly in a ship named the Argo, and after many adventures reached Colchis on the north coast of the Black Sea where they knew the Golden Fleece was kept. I was with them all the way, advising and protecting.

The King of Colchis, who owned the fleece, was suspicious of these strangers and their motives, and so he set the Argonauts three seemingly impossible tasks which they had to complete if they were to gain the fleece. What the king did not know was that his daughter, Medea, was helping them. I consider this one of my greatest feats: I made her fall in love with Jason. Medea was a young and beautiful witch with her own magical powers.

First, Jason had to plough a field with fire-breathing oxen, that he had to yoke himself. Medea provided an ointment that protected him from their dangerous breath. Then, Jason had to sow some dragon's teeth (given to him by the king) into the earth. The teeth sprouted into an army of hostile warriors, but Medea had previously told him how to defeat them. Before they attacked him, he threw a rock into the crowd. Unable to discover where the rock had come from, the soldiers turned on and killed one another until none were left. Jason's last task was to overcome the sleepless dragon which guarded the fleece. He sprayed the dragon with a potion distilled from herbs given to him by Medea. It fell asleep, and Jason was able to seize the Golden Fleece and bring it home, accompanied by Medea whom he vowed to love forever.

Unfortunately, the story of Jason, Medea and myself ends badly. When the Argonauts all returned to their homes, Medea was able to kill Pelias by a combination of magical power and trickery. As a result, Pelias's son drove Jason and Medea into exile for the murder, and the couple settled in Corinth where, in spite of all she had done for him, Jason abandoned Medea and married instead a daughter of the king. Medea retaliated by killing the two young sons she had borne by Jason. And because he had broken his vow to love Medea forever, Jason lost all favour with me, and died lonely and unhappy. He was asleep under the stern of the rotting Argo when it fell on him, killing him instantly.

It occurs to me, on reflection, that I seem to have spent rather too much time complaining about my husband's behaviour, so to compensate I will just finish by reminding the reader who I am – the Queen of the gods. I possess a natural authority and a deep feeling for order, ceremony and the honour of my family, the Olympians. This is why Zeus chose me, as the only goddess with enough presence and dignity to be his consort.

CHAPTER 4: APHRODITE

THESEUS AND HELEN

After her elder sister had left home to marry Agamemnon I heard nothing more of Helen – except about how news of her famous beauty was spreading across Greece. Soon after returning from my affair with Anchises, I happened to be visiting my temple in Athens, and it was then that I caught sight of her, arm in arm with Theseus on an Athens street. I made myself invisible and followed close behind them so as to hear their conversation. I soon realised that Helen had been kidnapped by him and taken to Athens. I knew that Theseus's latest wife, Antiope, had recently died. Was he seeking a new wife, I wondered, and had he chosen Helen after hearing the rumour about how lovely she was? I hoped so. A marriage between the Athenian hero and the woman said to be the most beautiful in the world seemed entirely appropriate. I soon discovered, however, that this hero had no thought of marriage and was merely planning to hold onto his prisoner until her father Tyndareus made him a suitable offer for her release. As Theseus smilingly explained to his prisoner, he was sure Tyndareus would agree because when the time came for her marriage he would certainly receive gifts from prospective husbands more valuable than any ransom.

I followed the couple back to Theseus's palace, and to the elegantly furnished bedroom he had provided for her. I couldn't accept that the Theseus I had known for all these years had become so mercenary, so indifferent to the power of love, so I decided to intervene. Every night I made him dream about Helen: her breasts, her thighs, her sexual allure, her availability while she slept in a bedroom so close to his. In his dreams I made him imagine how he would feel when her father paid the ransom and she had to leave him to marry someone else. As for Helen herself, I hardly needed to use my powers. She was already half in love with her handsome, articulate kidnapper. She enjoyed talking to him in the evenings and hearing stories about his life and adventures. And, although she was supposed to be his prisoner, she was allowed to enjoy all the luxury due to the guest of a king. All in all, she dreaded the day when a ship sent by Tyndareus would arrive at Piraeus, Athens' harbour, to take her back to Sparta.

After some weeks, envoys arrived from Tyndareus carrying the ransom of a hundred talents of gold that Theseus had demanded. They explained that very shortly a ship sent from Sparta would dock at Piraeus, and Helen would be escorted onto it. The next day we heard the ship had arrived and she was to be taken on board the following morning. That evening she went to her bed with tears in her eyes, knowing this was the end of her life in Athens. She did not want to go back to a stepfather who had never loved her, and who would certainly now blame her for all the money she had cost him. She would likely never see

Theseus again. She lay awake for hours until I sent her a sudden impulse that was too powerful for her to resist. Creeping quietly out of her room she made her way cautiously in the darkness to where she knew Theseus slept. I followed her down the corridor and into his bed chamber. She slipped off her night gown and, climbing into his bed, started stroking his cheek until he opened his eyes.

'Oh Theseus, I love you so much,' she whispered. She has prepared her little speech in advance. 'Please help me. Teach me how to express my love.'

He sat up and started to reply, but she stopped his mouth with a long kiss.

'This is our last night together. Can't we make it a night to remember for always?'

Dear reader, I hardly think I need dwell on the details of what happened next. My little plan had succeeded. Theseus abandoned the restraint and caution with which he had always treated his prisoner that night.   Neither of them gave a thought as to how the loss of Helen's virginity might affect her prospects of a future marriage, or about how Tyndareus might react if he ever found out. Helen got back to her own bed in the early morning to encounter Aethra, the mother of Theseus, who knew perfectly well where she had been.

It was time to say goodbye. Theseus told Helen that Aethra thought she needed looking after. She wanted to go to Sparta with her, and he had agreed.

'I will miss you, sweet Helen,' he told her, 'but I know one day you will find someone who loves you as deeply as you love them.'

By now I had decided to watch over Helen so I postponed any other projects I had, and became her constant companion, though I tried to make sure that

42

neither she nor Aethra were aware of my presence. The journey was uneventful, and Helen reached home to meet an angry Tyndareus, as she had anticipated. He told her that the ransom he had paid for her had almost bankrupted him, and she must compensate him for what he had lost. The only way to do that was for her to marry, and very soon he would be seeking suitors for her hand among the richest princes in Greece.

Within a few months of Helen's arrival in Sparta she started feeling rather ill, and her menses had ceased. She thought this was the result of missing Theseus, and the stress of worrying whom Tyndareus might choose as her husband, but Aethra soon realised she was pregnant. They needed to act fast because if the news got out the king's plans would be ruined, since beautiful young Helen would become damaged goods in the marriage market. Aethra went to Tyndareus and told him that she was finding it difficult to control Helen who was still behaving like a wilful child, too unruly to make a suitable wife. Aethra suggested that any marriage should be postponed, and that for the next six months Helen should be confined to the women's quarters in the palace, and kept under strict control. She must not be allowed to go outside or attend any feasts or festivals. This might make her grow up and learn obedience. Tyndareus welcomed Aethra's suggestion, and thanked her for volunteering to look after Helen during this period.

All this, of course, by no means solved the real problem: what to do when Helen actually gave birth. She refused to consider an abortion, which would sever her last link with the only man she had ever loved. I devised a plan and planted it into Aethra's mind, which she then discussed with Helen. She was to find a way to get Clymnestra,

Queen of Mycenae, to visit near the time that Helen was due to give birth, and then contrive to let her take the baby away with her without either Tyndareus or Clymnestra's husband, Agamemnon, knowing. So Aethra asked Tyndareus to invite his elder daughter to come and stay. She said Clytemnestra would be a good influence on Helen, and could instruct her on the duties and demands of a true wife, which she, being only a servant, could hardly do. Tyndareus, for whom Clytemnestra had always been his favourite child, was happy to agree with this. So the invitation was sent, and one day Clytemnestra arrived from Mycenae. Her appearance, however, was a real shock. Her eyes were red with crying and her body appeared swollen in the last stage of pregnancy. But when we asked when the baby was due she told us there was no baby. She had just suffered a most painful miscarriage. Agamemnon, of course, knew of her pregnancy but not about the miscarriage because he had been away from Mycenae during the previous fortnight preparing an expedition against pirates.

Clytemnestra told us that she was extremely unhappy. Agamemnon had treated her well at first but very soon had lost interest in her sexually. It had become a purely political marriage, or not even that because he never confided in her or invited her to any of his councils. All the privileges due to the Queen of Mycenae did not compensate for her sad and lonely existence. She had started to hate her husband and even hated the idea of giving birth to his offspring, a feeling which she suspected might have contributed to the miscarriage. Aethra and Helen felt extremely sorry for her, trapped in this loveless marriage, but they soon realised how her predicament might contribute to their plans.

At this point, the birth of Helen's child was imminent,

and Aethra started collecting everything we might need – medicines and drugs, linen for bandages, fresh olive oil, and above all a birthing stool which had to be borrowed from a local midwife whom they hoped could be trusted not to tell anyone why it was needed. These secretive preparations were made easier by the fact that Tyndareus was often away. He was busy mustering ships and crews so that he could join his brother Agamemnon in the campaign against pirates.

Clytemnestra was keen to help Aethra at the birth and they did a good job, especially to stop Helen screaming when the pain got too much. At last it was over, and little Iphigenia – the name Clytemnestra had given to the baby she had lost, and which we now gave to Helen's baby – was passed over to her mother briefly to hold in her arms. But all too soon Helen had to hand over the baby to her sister, who took her off to Mycenae in her carriage later that day. Helen never saw her daughter again. Not only had she lost the man she loved, but also his child.

When Tyndareus returned from hunting pirates he summoned Helen to interview. He said that now was her chance to repay the hundred talents of gold she had cost him. He was planning to invite all the eligible young nobles and kings of Greece to a two-week festival, after which one of them would be chosen as her husband. He explained that he wanted to retire soon, and as Helen's two younger brothers, Castor and Pollux, had already declined to take on the responsibilities and duties of kingship, and since her sister was already married, the inheritance of the throne of Sparta would fall to Helen's new husband. Tyndareus had no doubt that a large number of suitors would apply – though he failed to mention that it was her beauty that would be part of the attraction. He added that he was also inviting her cousin, Penelope, to join us for the festival. She was the daughter of his brother, Icarius, and was approximately the same age as Helen. Tyndareus said he hoped that Penelope's obedient and placid personality might be a guide for Helen and improve her own behaviour.

Tyndareus was right when he thought his invitation would be popular. No less than forty-five men with their servants eventually turned up, all of them bearing valuable gifts including horses and chariots, cattle and sheep, corn and wine. The suitors included Menelaus, accompanied by his brother, Agamemnon – not, of course, himself a suitor – as well as Idomeneus of Crete, Ajax of Salamis and Odysseus of Ithaca. As she got to know them all Helen decided she had no favourites, though Penelope was much taken with Odysseus who was articulate and amusing, unlike most of the rest. How Helen wished that Theseus had been among these suitors for her hand, but she knew that was impossible. We had recently heard that he had ceased to be King of Athens after a wave of unrest, and had retired to live out his days on the island of Samos.

The fortnight ended with a ceremony over which both Tyndareus and Agamemnon presided. Tyndareus said he knew that whoever was the winner, there would be bitter disappointment among the rest. Therefore he was asking all the suitors to swear a sacred oath that if anyone in the future were to try and abduct Helen from her chosen husband, then they would all combine to restore her to her rightful place. It was this 'oath of Tyndareus' which was to lead to the Greek invasion of Troy. After all the suitors had sworn the oath, it was Agamemnon's turn to speak, and to announce the winner. As most of them might have guessed by now, he announced that his brother, Menelaus, had won the competition. Agamemnon explained that the resulting alliance between the royal houses of Mycenae and Sparta – two sisters married to the two brothers of the House of Atreus – would give Greece the leadership it had always lacked, and that this was more valuable than all the generous gifts provided by the other suitors. So Helen was to marry Menelaus, and they would be King and Queen of Sparta as soon as Tyndareus retired.

One final event took place that day: Odysseus asked Penelope to marry him, and she accepted.

Helen was excited to become the new queen but she was less pleased when she had spent her first night with her new husband. Menelaus was nervous, and when he first saw his new wife naked seemed overcome by her beauty. It was as if he hardly knew how to proceed once they had embraced and kissed each other. At one point he did lay a hand on her breast, but then he left it there, apparently unsure what to do with it next. I was a hidden presence during this first encounter, and was somewhat shocked to witness the apparent caution with which they treated each other. Could it be that this new young king totally lacked sexual experience in spite of all the opportunities that must have come his way previously? He certainly seemed to lack initiative. I realised of course that Helen herself could not afford to take on the dominant role and teach her partner how to please her. She was supposed to have come to her marriage a virgin, and Menelaus would soon have accused her of previously making love to Theseus and no doubt to others.

Over the following nights Menelaus's sexual performance improved, but it still fell far short of what his new young wife had anticipated when she married him. And yet his pride that he had gained her as his wife was obvious. Her body belonged to him, and he was jealous of any man who so much as stared at her, let alone touched her.

There was the servant who carried perfumes and cosmetics to their room. For Menelaus he was a cause of anger and stress:

'I do not like the way he looked at you. He could not take his eyes off your body. I will not tolerate such behaviour in my palace.'

Then there was the driver who helped her step down from their coach:

'That man touched your breast when he lifted you down. Do not try to deny it, Helen, I saw it with my own eyes. I shall have him whipped.'

They had many bitter arguments along these lines during the first weeks of their marriage, some of them easily settled, others less so.

By far the worst quarrel took place early one morning when three soldiers entered Helen's bedroom without knocking, while she was having her hair done.

'We have come for the bronze, Your Majesty,' one of them said.

Another grabbed the mirror that Helen was holding and tried to wrest it from her, bruising her wrist in the process. They explained that the king had ordered them to search every room in the palace and collect up any items, however small, made of bronze. By the time they left, her private quarters had been ransacked, with ointments and cosmetics mixed up with hair pins and jewellery, the contents of bronze boxes, strewn across the floors.

When she had recovered from the raid, Helen went to confront her husband, but the explanation he gave her made things even worse, increasing her fury. Menelaus told her that, as well as peoples' homes, his brother had ordered all the Spartan temples to be plundered for the bronze that was needed to provide weapons and armour for a new raid they were planning. She couldn't forgive him for these acts of desecration, and neither could I. From now on she decided to quit his bed and sleep alone in the *gynacaeum*, the women's quarters of the palace.

This episode revealed two other aspects of Menelaus's personality: his love of violence, and his reliance on Agamemnon for guidance in all things. The brothers' greatest pleasure was planning and carrying out raiding expeditions against neighbouring states, or further afield by sea. Nothing, it seemed, could provide these two with the same pleasure in life as sacking a village or town, seizing its valuables and enslaving its inhabitants. The brothers of the House of Atreus were truly men of war, not of love.

That summer Menelaus received an embassy that visited him without warning from across the sea. It consisted of two well-born Trojan diplomats, both related to King Priam. This visit was to change not only the lives of Helen and her husband but that of many thousand other Greeks.

CHAPTER 5: APHRODITE

THE CONTEST

On the lower slopes of Mount Ida, not far from the walled city of Troy, a young shepherd named Paris was sitting watching his sheep. I had known Paris since he was a baby and now he was all grown up. He was exceedingly handsome, tall and slim with long black hair reaching down to his shoulders – like a young god in fact. A confident youth, he was a fast runner and so skilful with his bow that the local wolves and lions had learnt by experience to keep well away from him and his sheep.

Paris, however, was no ordinary shepherd. He was actually a royal prince, the son of Queen Hecuba and King Priam of Troy. The story goes that when he was born his mother was warned by a seer that if allowed to live he would one day be the cause of the city's destruction. When she told Priam about the dream, he gave the baby to his chief herdsman, Agelaus, with instructions to abandon him on the mountainside. Trojans take their dreams very seriously.

Either the baby was too pretty or the herdsman was too sensitive, but for whatever reason Agelaus kept Paris and brought him up as one of his own, with the constant warning never to enter Troy in case Priam still wanted him dead. He lived a peaceful and contented life as a shepherd and appeared to lack ambition. He married a charming nymph called Oenone. She had grown up in the forests of Mount Ida and was the daughter of a river god, and she had been given a special knowledge of medicine by Apollo.

As mentioned earlier, Paris's best friend was another young shepherd – my son, Aeneas. It was a curious coincidence that both Paris and Aeneas were related to the Trojan royal family, although only Paris was aware of the connection. As a child Aeneas had been looked after by local nymphs who, on my orders, never revealed who his parents were. And here he was, working as a cattle herder not too far from where Paris lived and worked. The two of them used to meet up almost every week.

Now I was to see Paris again, in most unusual circumstances. The story starts when, like all the other gods and goddesses, I was invited to celebrate the marriage of King Peleus and the sea nymph Thetis. It was held in a palace on the island of Aegina. All the Olympians were present together with lesser gods, nymphs and centaurs, all eating, drinking and enjoying themselves. At the far end of the hall, Zeus was sitting on his high throne, and on a sofa near him was his wife Hera. His daughter Athena and myself sat with Hera, but anyone could tell from our body language that we were not friendly despite sitting so close together.

In the middle of the revels I happened to notice Eris, the goddess of strife, enter the hall. This was odd because everyone knew she hadn't been invited in case she made trouble, as she so often did. But she was easy to recognise, with her angry expression and black wings folded behind her back. She was clearly angry at not being invited and out for revenge. She crept up to where we were sitting and rolled a little golden ball in our direction. It came to rest just beside my left foot.

I was intrigued and bent down to pick the ball up, but before I could, Athena grabbed it. She turned it round and found some writing: 'It says, *For the fairest, so* it must be for me.'

A rather childish argument ensued. I asked her several times to return my ball but she wouldn't.

'It isn't a ball, it's an apple with a stalk,' she said. 'Clearly it was meant for me, and now I've got it.'

'Only because you snatched it from me when I was bending down to get it. Give it back.'

Then Hera noticed us arguing and joined in. She grabbed Athena's hand and forced her to let go of the apple.

'Is this what you two are going on about? What a pretty toy! Most probably the writing on it refers to me and not you two at all,' she said. 'Perhaps we need someone to decide for us, and act as a judge. Where did it come from?'

I explained that I had seen Eris creep into the hall and deliberately roll the ball towards me, which meant it was mine. Realising the argument was going nowhere, Hera decided we should ask Zeus to decide. She turned round to look for her husband, but he had been listening to our quarrel and was clearly planning a quick exit.

'Don't run away,' Hera shouted at him. 'We've found a golden apple which claims to belong to the most beautiful. We'd like you to judge which of us that means.'

'How could I possibly judge between my wife and my two daughters?' he replied cautiously. 'I will find someone who can.'

The following morning a beauty competition for the

three of us was arranged at Zeus's request. We all prepared ourselves for it, though I do wonder whether either Athena or Hera really believed they had much chance of winning against me. I must admit I kept my magic girdle on when I first heard about the contest, although I did have to take it off later when Paris asked us all to undress.

The young shepherd was sitting on a rock surrounded by his sheep and thinking his thoughts, when suddenly he became aware of a small white cloud which came down out of the sky and descended to the earth just in front of him. Out of it stepped a well-dressed young man who had small wings attached to his sandals.

'I am Hermes, messenger of the gods,' the man said. 'I bring you a command from almighty Zeus. Will you kindly come with me.'

Paris found himself grasped by the elbow and steered into the cloud. Then the ground seemed to shift under his feet, the cloud disappeared, and he was in a different place, being stared at by three tall, elegant, beautiful women. Paris had never seen us before but he knew we were goddesses straight away and he had been in enough temples to guess who we were. Hera was the tallest, the one with the helmet was Athena, and the one with the tight-fitting dress was me.

Hermes introduced Paris to us. He asked Hera to give him the golden apple she was holding which she did, somewhat reluctantly. Then he showed Paris what was written on it, and what Zeus expected him to do:

'Each of these handsome goddesses claims that this apple belongs to her because each believes that she is the fairest. Your task is to decide who rightfully ought to have it.'

'Why me?' Paris asked. 'I'm only a shepherd and I really know nothing about goddesses.'

'But surely you do know something about female beauty,' I said. 'All you have to do is look at us carefully and decide. And please hurry up.'

Paris had an inspiration. He turned to Hermes.

'So this is really just a beauty competition. Can I be allowed to see a little more than their faces?'

'The rules of the contest are up to you,' said Hermes with a discreet smile.

Paris turned back to us.

'Please will you all take your clothes off.'

There was a pause.

'Do we really have to?' asked Hera. 'I didn't expect this.'

But it was too late. I had already undone the brooches which held my dress at the shoulders, and, as I wriggled, it slid down exposing my lovely breasts and thighs. Athena laid her spear down and copied me. Hera shrugged, then did the same. Slowly and voluptuously we all three twisted ourselves round while continuing to stare at Paris, who was starting to breathe a little faster.

Hera came up close to him. When she spoke, her deep brown eyes seemed to encapsulate the wisdom of the ages.

'Beauty in a goddess is not just about appearance, Paris,' she said. 'It's also about who she is, and what she can do. As you can see, I am beautiful, but what you can't see is my power. I am the wife of Zeus, and second in power only to him. If you choose me I will always be by your side. I can give you any kingdom in the world that you desire. I can make you lord of Asia or of Greece, and your subjects will bow before your will.'

Paris had no time to reply to this before Hera's place was taken by Athena, whose body came close to touching his, and whose penetrating grey-green eyes were so different from Hera's.

'I heard what she offers you,' Athena said, 'but have you considered how long you would stay on your throne if your enemies planned to invade and overcome you in battle? If you choose me I can make you win all your battles. I will always be your adviser and defender. As everyone knows, my helmet and my spear are the symbols of my eternal power on the battlefield. What do you say?'

Paris did not take long to work out a reply to both Hera and Athena. He thanked them for their offers, but then reminded them whom he was.

'I am only a shepherd boy,' he said, 'and I love my simple life. I don't want to be a king, with all the worries and problems they have. Also, I'm not a warrior, but a man of peace. I may be good with my bow, but I have no experience of swords and spears, the weapons of a hero. That sort of thing I leave to others.'

When he had finished speaking he became aware of a hand stroking his arm. It was me, Aphrodite, whom he had almost forgotten about but who was now standing, naked and irresistible, close by his side. Never in his life had he felt such sensuous excitement as at that moment.

'Dear Paris,' I said, 'would you like to know what I am offering you?'

I held up a small bronze mirror in front of his eyes and pronounced the name 'Helen'. A sudden vision briefly appeared in the mirror. It was of another naked young woman with long blonde hair and a swan-like neck above beautifully shaped breasts. The image seemed to smile and look directly at him.

'I can give you Helen,' I said, 'She is the Queen of Sparta, married to King Menelaus. She is rightly called the most beautiful woman in Greece.'

Paris hesitated. 'If she is married why should she agree to come away with me?'

'Leave that to me. Has no one told you about my powers? I will take you to her and make her fall deeply in love with you. Then she will leave her home and sail with you wherever you want. For all this I give you my sacred promise.'

This time Paris had no need to consider. Barely sparing a thought for his wife Oenone in the face of Helen's beauty, he nodded vigorously in agreement of my offer and handed me the apple. Then he turned to Hermes without looking at the other two goddesses.

'I've done what you asked,' he said, 'so would you kindly take me back to my sheep.'

Hera and Athena saw me take the apple. Without saying a word but with angry looks they both rose up into the air and floated away, probably to plot revenge on Paris and me. I knew they would both hate me because I had won the contest. I returned to Olympia to consider how best to carry out what I had promised, while Hermes guided Paris back to where he had first found him.

When I thought about it I realised there might be difficulties in my plan to link up the Queen of Sparta with a humble shepherd from the slopes of Mount Ida. After all, they had little in common, and also – how could Paris actually get to Sparta and meet Helen? Luckily, unexpected events made these problems much easier to solve. Agelaus, the king's herdsman and Paris's stepfather, was in charge of a huge white bull, much admired throughout the neighbourhood. One day officials from Troy came to his door and insisted on taking away this handsome animal so it could serve as the main prize at the annual festival of games that was due to be held outside the city walls.

Agelaus had long since made Paris swear that he would never enter Troy since if he did, King Priam might again demand the death he had been spared as a baby. Yet Paris, knowing himself a true athlete, hardened by an outdoor life, had always wanted to compete against those he saw as town-bred, pampered city youths. Now I put into his head that he could compete in these games, perhaps even become the *victor ludorum*, winner of the games, and so get back the white bull the officials had seized. I explained to him that his promise to Agelaus did not really count since the games were being held outside the city walls.

On the appointed day, he left his hut, having persuaded a friend to look after his sheep. Naturally I accompanied him – though invisible to all including Paris. A huge audience was already at the festival waiting to welcome the royal family. Paris saw the arrival of Hector and Deiphobus, Priam's two eldest sons, one of whom was expected to win the overall prize, as between them they had for several years dominated the rest of the field. But Paris, who had signed up to compete in various races as well as archery, spear-throwing and discus, won practically every event. Deiphobus, who during the day had become more and more irritated with this unknown 'peasant', finally lost all control during the wrestling when he found himself pinned on the ground with Paris sitting on top of him. Once freed, he whispered to his brother that Paris had uttered foul remarks about Priam and Hecuba, and then with drawn sword he grabbed his opponent by the hair, shouting that he deserved death. Suddenly a piercing voice from the crowd screamed out, 'STOP! He's your brother!' It was Agelaus who, learning from Paris's friend where he had gone, had decided to follow him. By now the king and queen were in the crowd and they heard the true story of how as a baby

Paris had escaped death on the mountain side, and been brought up by Agelaus as his step-son. Far from seeking Paris's death, Priam and Hecuba were now overjoyed by his survival, and they invited him to the palace to start a new life as a royal prince. He also was chosen *victor ludorum*, and picked the white bull as his prize.

Oenone was deeply upset when Paris told her he was leaving her in order to live in Troy as a member of the royal family but he easily put her out of his mind, obsessed as he was by the image of Helen he had seen in my mirror. He was welcomed to the palace by Priam and Hecuba, and even Deiphobus now seemed prepared to accept him as a brother. Priam held long conversations with Paris, instructing him as to the duties of a royal prince, and teaching him what he had never learnt as a simple shepherd, including the history of Troy and its royal family. It was mentioned, for instance, how several years earlier Telamon, the King of Salamis, had abducted Hesione, Priam's sister, to be his wife, and how she had never been allowed back to Troy. This gave me an idea, which I put into Paris's head. Why not suggest to Priam that he, Paris, lead an embassy to Salamis carrying valuable gifts? An enquiry could be made concerning Hesione's well-being, and with the suggestion that she might like to visit Troy to see her brother again, and meet all the nephews and nieces she had never seen. But once at sea they could sail to Sparta rather than Salamis. Paris passed on my suggestion and Priam was very taken with it. Within a few weeks a suitable ship had been prepared and an experienced crew chosen. Paris invited his friend Aeneas, who by now had also ceased to be a shepherd and was living in the city, to accompany him on the voyage. Aeneas said he didn't know anything about sailing but Paris said he didn't have to – they were to be diplomats, and others would sail the ship. So they set off from Troy, but once they were at sea Paris informed Aeneas they were going to Sparta, not Salamis. Within a week they had arrived and were shown to the palace of Menelaus.

CHAPTER 6: APHRODITE

FROM 'ABDUCTION' TO WAR

Paris and Aeneas were welcomed by Menelaus as ambassadors from Troy. As was the usual custom they were feasted and given beds for the night before discussing their business. The next morning a banquet was held at which the two Trojans were invited to explain why they had come to Sparta. Helen was present at the meeting, Menelaus telling his guests that it was normal in Greece for the wives of kings to attend when matters of state were discussed – though this was not the case in Troy, said Aeneas.

Paris explained about Priam's sister, Hesione, and how she had never returned to Troy after her marriage to Telemon, nor even sent a message about how she was getting on in Salamis. On questioning by Helen, Paris admitted they had no proof that Hesione was being held against her will, or even that she was unhappy. As to why it had taken several decades before Priam decided to investigate her fate, Paris said that it was only now that he had raised the issue with Priam and had himself volunteered to sail to Salamis.

Then he made his request: would Menelaus be prepared to join their expedition to Salamis and, if their invitation to Hesione to visit Troy was refused, to try and free her by force? If so, Priam promised to make new trading arrangements between Troy and Sparta which would be advantageous to both. A discussion ensued about the Salamis affair, but Menelaus eventually declined to get involved, arguing that at present Sparta had neither the ships nor the men to launch an attack on a powerful state like Salamis. The banquet ended with an invitation to Paris and Aeneas to stay in Sparta a few days. They were promised that everything would be done to make their stay as enjoyable as possible, and this offer was accepted with gratitude.

During the meal, it would have been clear to any onlooker that Paris was obsessed with Helen, even though she herself gave no acknowledgment of his attention. His shameless glances, loud sighs and bold signals must have caused her considerable embarrassment. He insisted on picking up her goblet and setting his lips to that part of the rim from which she had drunk. At one point she even found the words 'I love you, Helen!' traced in wine on the tabletop. She became terrified that Menelaus might suspect her of encouraging Paris's passion, but being an unobservant man he didn't. The only result of Paris's behaviour was that by expressing his feelings so crudely it made me realise what a simple and unsophisticated young fellow he was.

As the guests stood up to leave I felt it was time for me to carry out what I had promised. I gave a signal to my son Eros who had been waiting behind a pillar during the banquet. He now appeared, although invisible to the others, and following my instructions shot one of his magic arrows into Helen's breast as she left the hall. The result was obvious. As soon as she returned to her dressing room she started rhapsodising to her servant girls about the magnificent Trojan prince, his elegant clothing and god-like demeanour. Both Paris and Helen were now clearly love-struck. It only remained for me to invent a reason to get Menelaus away from Sparta – not an easy task – and my promise to Paris would be fulfilled.

I flew to Crete where Catreus, the elderly grandfather of Menelaus, lived. There I discovered that a young cousin of Catreus was planning to demonstrate his archery skills in a competition. I created an incident whereby Catreus was accidentally killed by a misplaced arrow while watching the competition. Messages were sent out to Agamemnon in Mycene and Menelaus in Sparta inviting them to Catreus's funeral. When he received the message Menelaus apologised to his guests and prepared to take his leave. 'I'm sorry to go but it is only fitting that my brother and I attend the funeral rites and games', he said. Then he departed after a ship had been prepared, promising to return as soon as he could.

'I hope you will both still be here when I get back,' he told them. 'I feel sure my wife will entertain you as I would wish.'

A few evenings after the king had left, Helen conducted Paris to the sacred grove and to the altar stone where once Zeus had swooped down on her mother in the shape of a giant swan. There, although hidden from passing eyes by the surrounding dense forest, they needed no torches since a full moon revealed their every movement to each other. Helen unclasped the brooches that held her *chiton* and let the fabric fall to her feet while Paris's fingers explored the contours of her throat and breasts. I watched while he entered her, showing a skill born of years of practice. To Helen the experience felt very different from her husband's often clumsy performances.

After their love-making Paris informed Helen that he planned to return home the following day, before Menelaus returned from his grandfather's funeral. He begged Helen not to say goodbye but to come with him to Troy. Now she was torn between her deep desire to love him and stay with him always, and her fear of a future in an unknown land with a man who had only just come into her life. I did my best to influence her dilemma, reminding her how little love there was left in her relationship to Menelaus. How could a marriage based merely on respect and propriety ever satisfy a passionate nature such as hers?

'Paris is offering you the chance to follow your deepest feelings,' I told her, 'and such a chance might never again arise in your lifetime.'

In the end I won, and she agreed to sail with Paris the next morning. Later, it was said she was abducted against her will, but that is not the truth. They spent the evening collecting some of her belongings from the palace storerooms and getting them packed ready to take down to the port of Gythium where Paris's ship was anchored. Again, some people have claimed that what they took was stolen from Menelaus's treasury but one has to remember that the king only acquired his wealth because he married Helen.

Having completed the funeral rites for Catreus, Menelaus and Agamemnon prepared to leave for their respective homes, but Menelaus asked his brother to come and stay in Sparta for a few days in order to meet Paris.

'I'm sure you'll like him,' he said, 'and anyway it's always good to keep up a friendship with Troy.'

They arrived to find the Trojans gone, and Helen with them. Both brothers were furious at this breaking of the bond of guest-friendship, so important among noble households, not to mention the vows of marriage which Helen had clearly betrayed. Agamemnon, as the king of the most powerful state in all Greece, saw Paris's conduct as an insult not just to Menelaus but to every patriotic Greek. He felt sure that Paris's behaviour had been prompted by Priam, and on reflection saw it as the perfect motive for leading an attack on Troy. It would be the trigger for invoking the oath of Tyndareus which so many prominent Greeks had sworn when they were suitors for Helen's hand. Therefore, as soon as he got back to Mycenae, Agamemnon sent out messages to all the Greek leaders asking them to join him with as many ships and men as they could manage in an invasion of Troy to rescue the abducted Queen of Sparta. He had long sought an excuse for this war since he wanted for himself the wealth that Priam acquired from charging every trading ship that entered the Black Sea. After all, argued Agamemnon, the Hellespont [*the Greek bridge*] should really belong to the Greeks, not Priam.

A vast fleet from all over Greece and its many islands gradually collected at Aulis, a Theban port which looked east across the Aegean towards Troy. Two important leaders did not at first appear. One was Odysseus who had been warned by an oracle that if he went to Troy it would be twenty years before he saw his homeland again. So he tried to act as if he had gone mad, but the messenger sent by Agamemnon to Ithaca soon discovered the truth and Odysseus had no alternative but to collect his ships and lead them to Aulis. It was the same with young Achilles, the greatest fighter in Greece. His mother, the sea-goddess Thetis, was gifted with second sight, and she warned her son that if he joined the expedition he would certainly be killed. She tried to hide him, disguised as a girl, among a group of other girls, but again the ruse was detected – this time by Odysseus himself – and Achilles had to join the rest at Aulis.

Finally, when everyone who was expected had arrived, all that remained was to wait for a favourable wind – Zephryus, the west wind – to blow, which would allow the fleet to set off in the right direction. But there was no wind at all and this calm went on for weeks. The stagnant heat led to disease spreading amongst the thousands of soldiers and sailors cooped up in the little port, and bitter anger filled their minds. Agamemnon knew that the anger was directed at him as commander-in-chief, and that his great project was verging on extinction. He called for Calchas, the Trojan seer who had earlier fled from Troy and entered Agamemnon's service. Calchas bowed low to the king but somehow seemed reluctant to speak. Only after repeated questioning did he reveal the problem they faced.

'Do you recall, Lord, that last week you went hunting in the forest south-west of here? I think at the time I reminded you that this was a grove sacred to the goddess, Artemis.'

'Well, what has that to do with anything?'

'You shot a white stag, did you not?'

'Get to the point, Calchas.'

'Unfortunately, this particular beast was also sacred to the goddess. She is very angry and seeks retribution, sire.'

It turned out that, as retribution, Artemis wanted Agamemnon to sacrifice to the goddess his teenage daughter, Iphigenia – or rather, the girl he and everyone else believed was his daughter although she was really the

65

daughter of Theseus and Helen. According to Calchas, Artemis had gone to Aeolus, keeper of the winds, and asked him to remove all wind from the port of Aulis until the required sacrifice had been made. Agamemnon was horrified at this proposal saying he was sure no god would have made such a barbaric demand, but after continued pressure from the entire Greek army, including even his brother Menelaus, he changed his mind.

To get Iphigenia to Aulis as soon as possible a pretext had to be invented. A messenger was sent to Mycenae to say that Achilles had asked for Iphigenia's hand in marriage, and that Agamemnon had agreed. Both Clytemnestra and her daughter were excited about this proposal and they set sail immediately. After their arrival at Aulis it was not until the last minute that they realised what was intended. Clytemnestra was overcome by her loathing towards the man prepared to murder his own daughter in order to maintain his own status and power, but she was powerless to stop it. Her eyes overflowed with tears as she hugged her beloved child while they waited for the fatal deed to take place.

Iphigenia, once she understood what was at stake, apparently said she was prepared to die for the sake of Greece but Clytemnestra never forgave Agamemnon, and she had to wait ten years to get her revenge. Achilles, too, was enraged when he heard that his name had been used to lure Iphigenia to her death, and this was the start of his hatred for Agamemnon which was later to disrupt the unity and morale of the entire Greek army. As for me, my existing hatred for Agamemnon and the House of Atreus only increased.

It was Calchas himself that Agamemnon instructed to be the executioner. Iphigenia was laid out on the sacrificial stone and Calchas cut her throat with a silver knife while calling out to Artemis to accept the sacrifice. A wind immediately started to blow among the trees that surrounded the sacred site – and not just any wind, but Zephyrus. Within days a thousand ships loaded with food and equipment of every kind had been dragged off the beaches and prepared for the high seas. The ships successfully found their way round Euboea and across the Aegean, but then I cast a spell which fogged the judgement of the pilot of Agamemnon's ship which was leading the fleet. Instead of sailing northwards past Lesbos and so to Troy he directed the entire fleet to turn towards the east when they had passed Chios so that they landed on the coast of Mysia in the mistaken belief that they had reached the mouth of the Scamander river near Troy. It was only after Greek soldiers had ravaged several Mysian villages – a forerunner of the brutal struggle that was to come – that the mistake was discovered and the fleet continued its journey to Troy. By this time word had reached the defenders of the city that enemies were approaching, and they had time to make their final preparations. Having beached their ships the Greeks built themselves a camp beside the sea, and the long war started.

CHAPTER 7: ATHENA

ATHENA AND THE GREEKS

I have always supported the Greeks. As I'm sure I've already mentioned, I am the divine patron of Athens, the city named after me. Visitors to Athens can see my great temple on the Acropolis from miles away. So when the fighting against Troy started I was there with my soldiers, and I gave them my support all during that ten-year war. Yes, ten years is a long time for a war, particularly as the Greek army, led by Agamemnon, was far larger and stronger than the Trojan army. The Greek forces also included many well-known heroes, the most famous of course being Achilles. The problem for the Greeks was Troy's massive walls, said to have been built by Poseidon and Apollo long ago when they were working for the Trojan king. So during those years of fighting we sometimes managed to push the Trojans right back to their own walls, but we never got inside the city.

Hera also fervently backed the Greeks, so she and I

tended to cooperate – though I must admit I didn't always like working with her. As Zeus's wife and sister she was rather too conscious of her standing, and much preferred giving orders to someone else (like me) rather than getting involved in the actual fighting. Also, our reasons for supporting the Greeks were slightly different. True, we both disliked Aphrodite, as well as Paris and Helen who were living in Troy throughout the war, and who had been brought together by Aphrodite in the first place. But Hera's other motive for wanting the destruction of Troy, which I certainly didn't share, was to annoy her husband. Zeus quite liked the Trojans as well as the Greeks, and he tried to be neutral between the two sides. At least he did until the last year of the war when things changed, as I will try and explain.

It was during this final year that a bitter argument started up between Agamemnon and Achilles. Agamemnon was of course the leader of the Greeks but everyone knew that Achilles was by far the best warrior in the army. Their quarrel was all about loss of honour. Agamemnon had been awarded a beautiful captive from the Trojans, as a prize of war. Unfortunately, her father was a priest of Apollo, and he came to the Greek camp to beseech Agamemnon to give her up and let her go back home. He refused, so the priest prayed to Apollo for help. Apollo heard his prayer and infected the Greek camp with a disastrous sickness that killed many warriors. A meeting of all the Greek leaders then took place in which Agamemnon reluctantly promised to give the girl back to her father, but on condition that he was given another prize instead, and the prize he wanted was a young princess named Bryseis who had been captured near Troy and awarded to Achilles as his special prize. Achilles, who was notoriously touchy about slights to his personal honour, shouted insults at Agamemnon and began pulling his sword out of its scabbard. This is where I stepped in. I covered myself in mist so no one could see me, and I stood just behind Achilles and grabbed him by his blond hair. I warned him to control his anger and put his sword away. My purpose here was to prevent a split in the Greek leadership which would have weakened their campaign. Achilles recognised my voice and reluctantly obeyed me.

The following morning two heralds were dispatched to Achilles's tent with orders to bring Bryseis to Agamemnon. Achilles did not try to stop them; instead, he went to see his mother, who was the nymph and sea-goddess Thetis, and told her the whole story. He said that since the commander-in-chief had insulted him by taking his war prize, he and his men would no longer take any part in the war. He asked his mother to go to Zeus and beg him to help the Trojans, so that when they started winning, Agamemnon would realise that he could not do without Achilles, and give Bryseis back. Zeus felt he had an obligation to Thetis because of the time she had released him from his bonds when all the other gods were plotting against him, so he promised to do what she asked, though he was worried what Hera would say when she found out. And somehow Hera, who hated the Trojans, did find out about his promise.

'Crafty one,' she said, 'I have a terrible fear that you have been won over by that nymph Thetis. I suspect you have promised her you will support the Trojans, which will bring death to many Greeks. Can this be true?'

Zeus merely told his wife it was none of her business to question his policies. Now however he was torn between appeasing Hera and doing what Thetis wanted. Day after day the war continued, and still Zeus hesitated over which side to support. But Achilles and his Myrmidons, as the warriors whom he had brought with him were called, remained on strike. They sat on the beach beside their ships while the rest of the Greek army fought on from dawn to dusk.

One morning Menelaus stepped forward from the Greek lines to make a suggestion.

'Greeks and Trojans alike have suffered much hardship because of my quarrel with Paris,' he said. 'Let he and I now fight it out alone. Whichever of us wins may carry Helen home as his wife, and the rest of us should make a solemn truce of friendship.'

His proposal was received with shouts of approval from both sides and the armies put down their weapons and sat down to watch, leaving a wide ring in which Menelaus and Paris could start their duel. However, the fight did not last long. Both of them flung their spears and missed. Then Menelaus ran up close to Paris, side-stepped his sword thrust and grabbed his helmet which he pulled, dragging Paris towards the Greek ranks and half strangling him with the cord round his neck. His death looked certain but Aphrodite, who was watching invisibly from above, managed at the last moment to descend, cut the cord and then whisk Paris away from the battlefield and back to Troy, leaving Menelaus grasping an empty helmet and storming round wondering how his opponent had vanished.

Meanwhile, in Olympia, Zeus called a council of the gods. He addressed them as follows:

'Just now Aphrodite has rescued Paris when his death was approaching. Therefore victory certainly rests with Menelaus. But, my friends, hasn't this war lasted long enough? Should we not now seal a pact between these foes?

If that were pleasing to all, King Priam's city might still stand, and Menelaus take Helen, his true wife, back to Greece.'

But Hera, in her bitter anger, answered him back:

'What's this you're saying, husband? Will you save Troy and thus render all my efforts null and void? All the toil and sweat I've suffered gathering an army from all of Greece to defeat Priam and his sons? Do as you wish but be clear – the rest of us disagree.'

Zeus was troubled by her words. 'My queen, how have Priam and his sons harmed you that you work so fervently to sack the sacred city of Troy? Come, please end this unnatural quarrel.'

Hera replied: 'I am Queen of the gods. Am I not allowed those feelings, those loves and hates, which even the lowest mortal may feel? I love my people the Greeks, and I support them against their enemies. How can this be unnatural?'

Her husband was silent for a moment, and then replied:

'Well then, my dear, do as you wish, so long as it ceases to be a source of strife between us.'

Hera then decided that if the truce had to be broken, might it at least be made to look as if it was the Trojans who broke it, and not the Greeks. She asked me to arrange this, so I went down in search of Pandarus, a Trojan whom I had been informed was an excellent archer, though not particularly bright. I spoke to him, disguised as one of his friends, and told him how pleased we all would be if Menelaus could be brought low by a well-fired arrow. No doubt Paris would award him valuable gifts for such an achievement. So Pandarus shot an arrow that would have found its target had not I deflected it at the last moment so that it merely scratched the surface of Menelaus's flesh. But this was enough for blood to flow, and he left the field to receive treatment. The treaty had now been breached and both sides grabbed their weapons and resumed the battle. Pandarus himself was in great danger as many Greeks had seen him shoot the arrow, and they converged on him from every side. But one of the finest of the Trojan warriors, Aeneas (who happened to be Aphrodite's son), tried to save Pandarus by driving his chariot up to him and inviting him to jump on board.

In Achilles's absence from the battlefield, my favourite Greek warrior was now Diomedes, an utterly fearless champion. I supported him, giving him special strength, and that day he slaughtered many Trojans. I took from his eyes the mist that usually covered a god, so that he could see both mortals and immortals. However, I did warn him never to make the mistake of openly challenging a god. But, I said, Aphrodite could be the exception.

'If you see her supporting the Trojans,' I told him, 'then you may stab her with your sword or spear. She is far from being an expert in human warfare.'

Writing this now I admit it was a foolish thing to say. I then asked Diomedes to search out and kill Pandarus who was now sharing the chariot of Aeneas, and he followed my instructions. When he saw Aeneas's chariot he threw a spear which I guided so that it hit Pandarus just below the eye. He crashed to the ground and lay dying. Aeneas leapt down to shield his body before the Greeks could rip off his armour and carry it away, as was the custom when an enemy was killed. But Diomedes seized a large boulder and threw it at Aeneas, smashing his hip joint. Aphrodite, who was constantly by her son's side, started to picked up his body but Diomedes came after her and stabbed her wrist with his spear. She screamed, dropped Aeneas, and fled up to Olympus to be comforted by Dione, her foster mother.

Meanwhile Apollo took Aeneas to safety and to receive divine treatment for his hip.

Zeus now remembered his promise to Thetis. He ordered all the other gods to stay away from the battle while he himself went down to help the Trojans. With his aid they pushed the Greeks back towards their camp and their beached ships. I went among them, in spite of Zeus's orders, and did my best to inspire their resistance, but the Trojans seemed unstoppable. Hector and a few of his warriors actually managed to break into the Greek camp and fight their way through to the beach where the Greek ships were drawn up. He could be seen running along the beach brandishing a burning torch with which he intended to set fire to the ships.

It was now that Hera thought of a way to turn the course of the war. Apparently she succeeded – I don't quite know how – in persuading Aphrodite to lend her the girdle she always wore, with its magical powers. Wearing this, she persuaded her husband to quit the battle and return with her to their palace in Olympia where they made furious love. Afterwards, Zeus fell into a deep sleep as Hera knew he would. And during his absence Hera and I succeeded briefly in once more rallying the Greeks, but all too soon Zeus awoke and he ordered us to leave the field of battle. In consequence the Trojans recovered their spirit.

The war then took another unexpected turn. Achilles's dearest friend, Patroclus, who had hitherto refused to join in the fighting, decided it was time to act before all the Greek ships were destroyed. He flung himself into the conflict, but soon found himself up against Hector and was stabbed in the heart. His death was the reason why Achilles himself now decided to break his strike and join the war, and he set off in pursuit of Hector, seeking revenge for the killing of Patroclus. This in turn meant that Zeus no longer needed to do what Thetis, the mother of Achilles, had begged him to do, and support the Trojans. Zeus therefore decreed that from now on any of the gods might support whichever side they wanted, while he watched. He sat on the summit of Mount Ida, and viewed the bloody conflict in which both gods and mortals were soon involved.

On the Trojan side was brutal Ares, god of war, and when he saw me he tried to wound me in the stomach with his long bronze spear. But I was wearing my tasselled *aegis*, a garment that no spear or sword could penetrate. I picked up a huge black stone which once marked the boundary of a field, and with it I hit him on the neck. He fell to the ground sobbing, and Aphrodite, who had once been his lover, picked him up and tried to carry him away to safety. I ran after her and dealt her a blow on her breast. She collapsed, and for a time both she and Ares lay on the ground groaning, until they recovered enough to flee up to Olympus.

With help from both Hera and myself, the Greeks forced the Trojan army away from their ships and then back across the plain towards the walls of Troy. Achilles was on the rampage, cutting his way through the ranks of the enemy and leaving a trail of the dead and dying behind him. He was backed up by his Myrmidons who stripped the armour from the Trojan bodies as a prize of war. Many Trojans turned and ran, some to hide inside the city, others to the Scamander river which soon became choked with dead or wounded warriors. and where red blood stained the water. Still wearing his armour, Achilles leapt into the river in pursuit of those who were trying to hide from him, but the river god, who was angry with him for polluting his river, sent great waves to drown him. If I had not been just behind

75

Achilles he would certainly have drowned. I lifted his shoulders above the rushing water and pulled him to the bank.

Then Achilles returned to the city walls in search for Hector, the man who had killed his dear friend, and eventually the two met in front of the Scaean gates. Hector was terrified when he saw his mortal enemy, and he ran round the walls with Achilles in close pursuit. But I adopted the form and voice of Deiphobus, one of Hector's brothers, and I told him to stand up and fight, and that I would be by his side. This boosted Hector's spirit and he turned to face his adversary. First he asked Achilles to promise that if he won he would allow his enemy's dead body to be taken back by his friends for burial and not left for the dogs and birds to eat. He would promise the same if he won the duel.

Achilles scowled at him and shouted, 'Make me no appeals, you madman. There can be no treaties between lions and men, or between wolves and lambs, and the same goes for you and me. I wish I could devour you myself, cut you in pieces and eat your flesh raw for all the harm you have done me.'

He then let fly his spear which would have struck Hector's forehead had he not ducked just in time. The spear fixed itself in the earth, and I pulled it out and gave it back to Achilles. Then Hector threw his own spear which was deflected by Achilles's mighty shield. It was his only spear so he turned to Deiphobus and asked him for another. But Deiphobus was not there, and now Hector realised a god had tricked him, and that death was close. Then the two charged towards each other with swords drawn. Achilles looked over Hector's body to find a vulnerable place and saw flesh between armour and helmet, just where the collar bones hold the join of neck and shoulders. There he plunged his sword. And death enfolded Hector, and his spirit left his body and made its way to Hades, weeping for its fate.

I was happy that this great Trojan leader, who had done so much harm to the Greeks, was now no longer among the living, yet I cannot say I approved of how Achilles now proceeded to treat Hector's body. He stripped him of his armour, then cut through the flesh round the tendons of both feet, attaching ox-hide straps which he tied fast to his chariot. Mounting the chariot, he dragged the body round the city walls so that Hector's once handsome head was bruised and buried in dust. And many Trojans, including Priam and Hecuba, Hector's parents, wept, as from the ramparts above they witnessed the death of their son and the defilement of his body. But Achilles himself had not long to live. The very next morning he was killed by an arrow shot by Paris from the ramparts of Troy. It was a sad, undignified end to this mighty warrior, who would have easily defeated the cowardly Paris in any fair and even contest.

The Greeks had lost their greatest hero, and yet within weeks of Achilles's death they succeeded in entering Troy and burning the city to the ground. Believe me when I say: this victory was due to me and no one else. I gave Odysseus a dream in which I advised the construction of a huge wooden horse in which Greek soldiers could be hidden after the rest of the army pretended to sail away back to Greece. Not only that, but in the dream I also suggested how the Trojans might be persuaded to transport the horse into Troy so that the soldiers inside could leap out in the night and open the gates for the rest of the Greek army to enter the city. This involved recruiting a Greek named Sinon to act as a spy. Sinon appeared to the Trojans when

77

they were investigating the horse and claimed he had been due to be sacrificed to the gods so that the Greek ships might sail home under a favourable wind, but had managed to escape from his imprisonment. Sinon also told the Trojans that the horse had been built in my honour, and he suggested that if they pulled it into Troy and left it beside my temple, then I would certainly start supporting the Trojans instead of the Greeks.

The only thing I disagreed with in Sinon's speech was that the sacrifice was supposed to be to me. I would never have asked for a human sacrifice, and Odysseus invented that bit. Otherwise, everything went according to my suggestions. Odysseus explained my plan to Agamemnon, the horse was built and left on the beach with Greek soldiers hidden inside it, the Trojans believed Sinon's story, the horse was pulled into the city, and the final result was the destruction of Troy and the fall of the house of Priam.

It was after their triumph that the victors seemed to have forgotten to give those gods who had supported them throughout the war the thanks and honour due to them. Not only did they fail to honour us but they desecrated our temples in the city, searching for Trojans who had sought sanctuary inside them. The worst example of this behaviour was when Ajax (the lesser), a prominent Greek leader, entered my temple to discover the Trojan princess Cassandra clinging to my statue. He dragged her away and raped her. No Greek protested at his behaviour and it was then that I became determined for vengeance.

CHAPTER 8: APHRODITE

APHRODITE AND THE TROJAN WAR

After years of bitter fighting between Greeks and Trojans there still seemed no end to this unhappy war. By now many of the Olympian gods were openly joining in, giving advice to the side they supported or even using swords or spears themselves. On the Greek side there was Poseidon, Zeus's brother, and also, of course, Hera and Athena. Supporting the Trojans were myself, Apollo (who loved and admired the Trojan leader, Hector), and also Ares, god of war and my sometime lover.

Ares' support was vital for the Trojans, yet I admit that his coarse brutality and love of inflicting pain did not endear him to me. Zeus himself could not decide what his best policy was. He was fond of Troy whose rulers had always shown him honour and respect, yet he also greatly admired the leaders of the Greeks, in particular, Achilles and King Agamemnon. As usual, he also wanted, if possible, to avoid confrontation with his forceful wife who was determined to see the Trojans defeated, and their city reduced to ashes.

War is usually told as a narrative about heroes – a very limited kind of story. What is a hero? Someone good at killing people. In the case of the Greeks in this war, it is someone who has chosen to leave his family to sail far from home in order to kill strangers, and if possible burn a city to the ground. I hate the fighting and everything to do with it – the screams of the wounded, the mutilated bodies lying in the mud, the shout of satisfaction when a spear penetrates some victim's stomach. I would have happily remained throughout the war in my palace on Mount Olympus, far from the battlefield. But I had a duty to try and watch after those I loved – my dear son Aeneas, and, to a lesser extent, Paris and his wife Helen. So I spent hours each day watching from above, wrapped in a dark cloud so I wouldn't be seen.

Early one morning, when the combat between the two sides seemed particularly fierce, I caught sight of Paris wearing his leopard skin over his shoulder and shaking a pair of bronze-capped spears. He was strutting in front of the Trojan ranks shouting insults at the Greeks and challenging any of their best men to fight him, one to one. When Menelaus, who was in his chariot, noticed Paris he immediately jumped down and ran towards him. Paris saw him coming, and shrank back into the Trojan ranks. This was typical of Paris who, although boastful, was never as confident as he made out. But Hector, leading warrior of the Trojans, when he saw Paris hiding in the middle of the Trojan army, came up and taunted him.

'Oh Paris my brother, you are the one who started this war. If you now refuse to stand up to King Menelaus whom you have wronged, whose wife you stole and brought to our city, then there will be no help for us in your lyre playing, your long hair and your pretty looks.'

Paris was ashamed, and replied, 'Hector, what you say is not unfair. If you want me now to face Menelaus in single combat, have the others sit down and form a circle, both Trojans and Greeks. Whichever of us wins can have Helen, and the rest are to stop fighting and make a solemn truce of friendship.'

When both sides heard about this offer from Paris they were overjoyed and started taking off their armour, thinking this was the end of the misery of war. And the duel started, watched from above by myself, and also by Athena who was certain of Menelaus's victory.

Both Paris and Menelaus flung their spears and missed their targets, but then Menelaus rushed towards Paris, seized him by his helmet and started dragging him backwards towards the Greek line, throttled by the helmet strap round his neck. If I had not intervened, it would have been certain death for him. I flew down and quickly broke the strap, leaving Menelaus to stagger back clutching an empty helmet. I wrapped Paris in a thick mist, carried him off the battlefield and set him down in his own bedroom in Troy. Then I found Helen who was in her room weaving a tapestry that told the story of the war. I told her about the duel and I took her to Paris who was still shaking with fear, thinking about his narrow escape. Helen did not seem particularly pleased to see him and addressed him with bitter words.

'So it seems you are in hiding, you coward. How many times have you boasted to me that you were superior to him, and now we see the truth.'

But I used my skills to draw them towards each other just as I have done with so many other mortal couples. Soon they had stripped off their clothing and were lying on the bed making love. Meanwhile, back on the field of battle, Menelaus was raging up and down the mass of troops wondering what had happened to his opponent.

Agamemnon stood up and addressed the warriors of both sides: 'Listen to me, both Trojans and Greeks. Victory plainly rests with my brother Menelaus, so now I suggest that Helen is restored to her former husband and a fitting be price paid for her abduction from Mycenae. These must be the terms for a lasting treaty between our two sides.'

And everyone who heard him applauded. But Hera and her obedient servant Athena were angry. They wanted the total destruction of Troy, not a treaty that would leave the city intact. So Athena persuaded Pandarus, a renowned Trojan archer, to break the treaty by shooting an arrow at Menelaus which wounded him slightly – just enough that he had to quit the battlefield, and this immediately led to a resumption of the fighting.

Zeus now ordered all the other gods to stay away from the battlefield, while he himself lent his support to the Trojans as he had promised Thetis that he would. As a result the Greeks were forced back almost to their ships, while Hera and Athena could do nothing but watch. There was rejoicing in the Trojan camp that night but despair among the Greeks. Agamemnon was even for giving up the campaign entirely and sailing back to Greece, although Nestor, oldest and wisest among their leaders, suggested instead that one more attempt be made to persuade Achilles to return to the war – which Agamemnon did, but still in vain.

Hera had one more trick up her sleeve. She adorned herself in all her finery, and then she came to my palace in Olympia to ask if she could borrow the magic belt which I always wore under my dress. I was surprised to receive such a request from Hera, who had been so hostile to me since our contest. The only other time she had ever asked for my help was years earlier, when I had lent her my son Eros to make Medea fall in love with Jason, but now I listened to the long story she told me about why she needed the belt. The gist of the story was that Oceanus and Tethys, the Titans who had brought Hera up when she was young, had quarrelled, and were now living apart from each other. So Hera, who loved them both, wanted to visit Oceanus in his palace at the edge of the world, and make him wear the belt in order that that he might become attractive again to his estranged wife.

Knowing Hera as I did, I wasn't entirely sure I believed this tale but she was so charming to me that I eventually lent it to her, which turned out to be a great mistake. She asked me to undress so as to see how the belt fitted. Then she undid it and started gently stroking my breasts. She cried, 'Oh Aphrodite, you're so beautiful. I can't see how you could ever need a magic belt to attract someone.'

I said, 'It's a bit difficult to put on the first time. Take your clothes off and let me show you.'

Quite soon we were kissing and holding each other. (Although I hated her support of the Greeks I have always admired her body.) When we had finished she asked me more about the belt: where had I got it, and how easy was it to make the magic work. I explained that Hephaestus and I had collaborated in his workshop to make it, and that it was quite easy to use. All you had to do was look the person you wanted to attract straight in the eye and concentrate very hard. Then she asked me a slightly awkward question: had I been wearing the belt when Paris was judging which of us three goddesses was the most beautiful? I admit now that I did have it on when the contest started, though I had secretly taken it off when we were all asked to undress – so of course I said no. If I had said yes she would have told everyone how unfair the contest was, and that was why she had lost.

Of course, I found out later that the story she gave me was completely untrue, and she instead used the belt to seduce Zeus and send him into a deep, satisfied sleep so she and Hera could help the Greeks. Luckily, Zeus woke up just in time. When he saw the Trojans in disarray and their great leader Hector lying unconscious on the ground having been hit by a stone, he soon guessed who had cheated him. He ordered Athena and Hera to stay away from the battle, and this time he threatened to beat Hera if she disobeyed him. Once more, the Trojans started winning, and this time Hector very nearly reached the Greek ships which he was planning to burn.

When Hector died Paris became Priam's oldest surviving son, and therefore heir to the Trojan kingdom – although there were still many Trojans who, believing that the war was entirely his fault, could not accept his new status. Paris and his wife Helen were still in love, and one night she told him a story she had heard about Achilles: when he was a baby his mother Thetis had dipped him in the river Styx to make him invulnerable. However, she had been interrupted by her husband Peleus who thought she was trying to kill their baby. Consequently, Achilles's left heel where she had been holding him was never dipped in the river.

'For an archer like you,' Helen said to Paris, 'no target is too small, so if you ever get the opportunity …'

Paris did not wait long before acting on the advice Helen had given him. The following day I was watching Achilles hacking and slashing his way through the Trojan ranks just as he had done every morning. Suddenly I noticed Paris on the Trojan ramparts, his bowstring drawn, waiting for his chance. It came when Achilles raised his left foot in order not to stumble over the body of a dead Trojan. The arrow shot by Paris struck the side of the foot, just above the heel and below the grieve of his armour. Achilles roared in pain and crashed to the ground, lying motionless while others surrounded his body to prevent the Trojans from stripping off the armour. The great warrior was soon dead, and when the Trojans heard how he had died, Paris was hailed as a true hero, and no longer someone hateful who was guilty of causing the war by stealing the wife of a Greek king. When Paris met his mother, Queen Hecuba, instead of ignoring him as she had in the past, she hugged and kissed him, and he realised that he was now accepted by all as King Priam's true heir.

Sadly, neither Paris's new status, nor his life, lasted very long. A few days later he found himself in a duel with a Greek warrior named Philoctetes who, as an archer, had a major advantage over Paris. This was that he possessed the bow and arrows which had once belonged to the mighty Hercules. As a young man Philoctetes had been the constant companion of Hercules, who had passed on to him his semi-divine bow with arrows that could penetrate any armour. Now, an arrow from Paris flew straight for Philoctetes but failed to penetrate his breast plate, whereas the arrow shot simultaneously by Philoctetes, which I suspect was guided by Athena, lodged in Paris's chest, causing him to collapse onto the ground. His wounded body was snatched up by his companions and taken into safety while Helen, who had been watching the encounter from the ramparts, rushed down to his side. She managed to remove the arrow and staunch the blood, but Paris, drifting in and out of consciousness, could speak only one word, his first wife's name: 'Oenone'. Paris had once told Helen that Oenone possessed divine powers of healing, a gift from Apollo, so word was sent for her to come as fast as she could. For hours Helen prayed to me, begging me to save her husband, but there was nothing to be done against the magic power of an arrow from the bow of Hercules.

Then came the news: Oenone would not come. She could not forgive the way Paris had deserted her, but later, when she heard that he had died, she killed herself. Naturally, I felt guilt concerning the fate of this young nymph since I know she loved Paris deeply. His leaving her was my fault because I encouraged him to seek out Helen.

Not long after Paris's death came the famous episode of the wooden horse, a cunning piece of trickery organised by Odysseus – probably with some help from Athena. The plan involved the Greek army pretending to go home when in fact they had landed behind the nearby island of Tenedos. They left behind them an enormous wooden horse in which thirty warriors were hidden. When the Trojans arrived to inspect the horse they were spun a complicated story by Sinon, a Greek, who alleged he had been awaiting execution for certain crimes but had managed to escape. Sinon explained that the horse had been built in honour of Athena, and how pleased she would be if it was taken into Troy and parked beside her temple. He was believed, and the horse was pulled into the city, but that night the Greek warriors crept out of it and opened the Scaean gate to allow the rest of the Greek army to enter and lay waste the city. The plot had been successful, and beautiful Troy was no more.

Before that happened I had made my last attempt to save

Troy. I knew that Helen had a special skill for mimicry, so I sent her a vivid dream in which she learnt the truth about the warriors hidden in the horse. She was told to leave her bed, make her way to Athena's temple, then stand beside the horse and call out to some of the Greek leaders in the voices of their own wives.

'Odysseus, my darling, it's me. It's your Penelope. Yes, I am here. Climb down quickly. I have something important to tell you.'

But there was no reply, and eventually Helen returned home, deciding that her dream must have been a false one.

Before dawn the Greek army had started their work of murder and devastation. As for me, I was by now the only god left supporting the Trojans so there was little I could do. Apollo had retired to Olympia following the death of Hector, his favourite Trojan, and Ares had changed sides and started to help the Greeks after he was wounded in battle. All that remained for me now was to try and help my son, Aeneas, and also Helen, to escape with their lives.

I might just add that the war might have ended far sooner than it did had it not been for Hera's hatred of Helen and poor Paris. An honourable peace could easily have been agreed between Priam and Agamemnon. But no, Hera and her servant, Athena, were determined to continue the fighting until Troy had been totally destroyed.

CHAPTER 9: ATHENA

FROM WAR TO CALYPSO

I supported the Greeks throughout their war against Troy but I couldn't forgive their behaviour after the war ended – especially the way Ajax (the lesser) dishonoured me by raping the Trojan princess Cassandra in my temple where she had sought sanctuary. After that I foolishly went to Poseidon and asked him to help me punish them all by making it hard for them to sail home. He readily agreed, and sent powerful storms that blew them all off course. Ajax himself drowned.

You might ask: why Odysseus? It is true, I had always shown him and his family affection, and in the war I protected him from his enemies. I saw him as the cleverest of the Greek leaders. Plus with his humour and his schemes he was never dull. But I could not forget what he did before the destruction of Troy. He and his friend Diomedes managed to enter the city by a secret tunnel, and then steal my image, the sacred *palladium*, from my temple. Almost as bad as what Ajax did later. And many of his other seemingly brilliant ideas actually came from me. For instance, the Trojan horse. I suggested that in a dream I gave him. Left to himself Odysseus was never so original. So when it came to punishing the Greeks I felt no inclination to make him an exception.

Poseidon made sure that Odysseus had a difficult time after he left Troy. One place where the twelve ships of his fleet managed to land was at Ismarus in Thrace, the home of the Cicones. Here the Greeks behaved with the same greed and brutality as any pirates, sacking the town and killing many of its citizens, as well as seizing some younger women along with what valuables they could get their hands on. Afterwards they celebrated their cruelty much of the night, roasting sheep and cattle along the beach and getting drunk on the local wine. This was one occasion when Odysseus failed to discipline his men, and retribution came swiftly. When first attacked, the Cicones had called out for help to neighbouring tribes, who were strong and numerous. At early dawn these seasoned warriors descended on the Greek ships, some on horseback and others on foot.

Six of the crew from each ship died in the long battle that followed. The rest managed to sail away, feeling lucky to be alive and grieving for their lost friends. After they left Ismarus, they soon lost all track of where they were. Powerful winds released by Poseidon blew them southwards for many days and nights without any sight of land. Finally they came across a country completely unknown to them, and it was here that Odysseus made his biggest mistake, although I must admit it was also here that he showed how cunning he could be in a really disastrous situation.

The Trojans beached their ships and camped for the night. Across a narrow strip of water they could see more land which appeared inhabited, as columns of smoke were rising from it. The next morning, leaving most of his companions to await his return, Odysseus set out with twelve men in his own ship to explore this unknown country. He took with him a goatskin full of wine in case he needed to reward anyone they might meet who offered them hospitality. They tied up the ship and wandered along the beach until they came across a huge cave which contained crates of cheese and pens full of young goats and lambs. Clearly their owner was out with his flocks on the hills above. Odysseus's men wanted to take what they could carry and get back to their ship as fast as possible but he refused, and insisted they wait until the owner returned, hoping he would give them gifts. However, when the owner did arrive with his goats and sheep he turned out to be rather less hospitable than Odysseus had hoped. This was Polyphemus, a fearsome Cyclops. He rolled back a gigantic boulder to seal up the mouth of the cave, and then seized two sailors and proceeded to eat them raw.

There was nothing anyone could do. They remained prisoners for the night and all the next day, Polyphemus devouring two more of the sailors for breakfast and another two when he returned from looking after his flocks. But that evening Odysseus devised a plan. He offered Polyphemus several glasses of strong wine until he fell into a drunken slumber. Then, having sharpened the end of a huge wooden stake in the fire, several of the men drove the red-hot spike into the Cyclops's single eye, and twisted it. Bellowing with rage and pain he sprang up, pulled the spike out of his eye and rushed round the cave trying to find his tormentors, but since he was blind they were able to avoid him. However, they still had to escape from the cave. If they killed Polyphemus they might find themselves imprisoned forever as no one except him could possibly shift the boulder covering the entrance. Odysseus's solution was for each sailor to choose three large rams, bind them together with thin strips of bark, and then get themselves tied up under the middle ram. Early the next morning Polyphemus moved the boulder and then sat at the cave entrance checking his sheep and goats as they left the cave. But he only moved his hands across their backs to make sure none carried a man, and he never thought to check underneath. Once out of the cave they all ran back to their ship and started to row out to re-join the others. Polyphemus flung an enormous rock in their direction which nearly capsized them, but the rock itself missed the ship, and they were free.

However, before they had rowed far, Odysseus in his foolish pride decided to clearly identify himself by shouting out to Polyphemus as they rowed away: 'Cyclops! If any mortal asks you how you lost your eye, say it was done by Odysseus from Ithaca, the city-sacker!'

Polyphemus now knew who had wounded him and he prayed to his father Poseidon for revenge, beseeching him that Odysseus never reach his home, or if he did, that he should reach it alone and in pain, having lost all his men. The main results of this encounter were therefore that not only did he lose six more of his companions but also that it increased the hostility of Poseidon, who by this time might well have left Odysseus and his ships alone if he hadn't blinded his son.

The fleet was now blown northwards by Poseidon's storms for long days and nights until they came across yet another land unknown to Greeks. They saw signs of habitation and the narrow entrance to a harbour protected on all sides by cliffs. This was when Odysseus made his most costly mistake so far as the lives of his comrades were concerned. The crews of all his ships, exhausted after hours of rowing against hostile winds, entered the calm of the harbour, hoping to receive hospitality from the people of this land. Only Odysseus avoided the harbour entrance, fastening his ship's ropes to a rock some distance away. Perhaps he was suspicious of the kind of welcome the others might receive. Clearly. however, he was not suspicious enough to stop them from going.

Odysseus sent three of his men to discover who these people were. They came across a tall young girl out fetching water. She failed to understand their language but took them to the high-roofed palace of the king who was a giant, taller even than Polyphemus. As soon as he saw them he tried to kill them and started to eat one of them. The others escaped and ran back to their ship. Odysseus immediately cut the ship's ropes, and the rowers bent to their oars. But from the harbour they could hear the uproar of ships being smashed by boulders flung from the cliffs above, and the screams of dying men, speared like fish. Only Odysseus and his crew escaped from Laestrigonia, that other land of cannibal giants.

They were finally washed up on Aeaea, the island of the sorceress, Circe, who was the daughter of Helios, the sun god. I had met and chatted to Circe a couple of times at receptions given by her father in his palace on the edge of the world. This was when she was a shy and youthful nymph who preferred listening to her seniors rather than expressing her own opinions. Later, I heard she had been punished because she had offended her father, and also Zeus, by claiming to possess special powers derived from the earth and the plants that grew on it. She had boasted to her father that she could brew a potion that could change fish into birds, or humans into animals. In other words,

Circe had become a witch. Such behaviour always angered and frightened the Olympian gods who saw it as a challenge to their divine status. So Helios had consulted Zeus, and between them they had decided to expel Circe to this remote and uninhabited island where she could do little harm to the rest of the world. But Helios at least made sure that life on the island for his daughter would be consonant with his own status as a superior god. I knew that the house to which she had been expelled, and where she would invite Odysseus, was a magical house full of elegant furniture, where the floors were always clean, the beds made themselves, and in the kitchen food and wine were always replenished.

By now I felt it was time I visited Odysseus. I also thought I'd like to see Circe's house for myself, and see how much the young nymph I had once known had changed. So I hid myself in a mist and went down to Aeaea where Odysseus's men had beached the one ship they had left, and were discussing what to do next. They had noticed smoke curling into the air above the treetops but after their experience with the Laestrigonians were reluctant to explore further. Finally, Odysseus decided to send half his crew off to investigate while he remained on the beach with the rest. I followed them along narrow pathways up a hill and through the woods until they came to a clearing with a large house in the middle. Inside it they could hear a woman singing. They plucked up their courage and knocked on the front door. Circe opened it and invited the men to join her in a meal. All entered except their leader, Eurylochus, who stayed outside, clearly anticipating a trap. Invisible, I went in with the others and watched as she plied them with food and with dark red wine which I realised was drugged. When they had eaten she went among them, tapping each with her wand. Their ribs cracked, their legs shrivelled, then they fell on all-fours and turned into pigs. She drove them out of the back door and into a large pen where other pigs were already held. Clearly she had done this sort of thing before.

I left Circe's house and returned to the top of the hill, from where I could see the beach. Eurylochus, surrounded by a crowd of sailors, was obviously trying to explain what he had seen, and how his comrades seemed to have suddenly disappeared after their meal. Then I saw Odysseus strapping his sword to his back and striding off. I knew he was coming in search of his men, and I guessed that all the others had refused to go with him. This was the moment I decided I must help him and, knowing what witches were like, I had already made certain preparations. Dissolving the mist which had hidden me, I transformed myself into an adolescent boy out hunting with his bow and arrows and his leather satchel. There was a fallen tree trunk near the path Odysseus was bound to take, so I sat on it and waited for him to appear.

He saw me as he came up the path so I called him over.

'I saw you arrive on the island,' I told him. 'You must be Odysseus. My mother has told me all about you. You are going down to visit the witch in the big house, aren't you?'

He was taken aback. 'And who might you be?'

I spun him a story. 'My name is Tyro and my mother is a sea nymph. She lives over there on the other side of the island. She told me to give you this.'

I took a bag from my satchel and handed it to him. Naturally he was suspicious. I explained it was a bunch of very rare flowers called moly, which had the power to stop any spell taking effect. I told him my mother had been brought up on the island and knew every plant and what it could do. Luckily, she had come across a small group of

94

moly plants in the deepest part of the forest. (Actually, I had picked these on the slopes of Mount Dicte in Crete. There were none on the island.) Then I told him how dangerous Circe was, and how she enjoyed changing her visitors into animals, using herbal potions and her magic wand. She had already turned half his crew into pigs, and would do the same to him given half a chance. He must keep the moly close beside him, smelling them from time to time, and then at the right moment threaten to kill her if she refused to change his men back again. I explained that the reason we wanted him to defeat Circe was that my mother hated the way some of her pigs kept escaping from their pen and then crashing round the island, damaging the plants. Odysseus took the bag and asked me to give his grateful thanks to my mother, but I could see he half-suspected I was not what I said I was.

Odysseus was welcomed by Circe, and later I heard that things happened just as I had predicted. He told her about his adventures and about the anger of Poseidon, all the while pretending to sip the goblet of wine she gave him.

When she suddenly tapped him with her wand, crying out, 'Now I'm afraid you must go join your fellows in the back garden!' he jumped up and threatened her with his sword. It seems she was so astonished he had avoided her spell that she suggested they should seal an agreement by moving to her bedroom. Then she swore an oath on the river Styx that she would never again try to harm him, and after they had made love she changed all the pigs back into humans. The others waiting near the ship were also summoned and invited to stay.

Days became weeks and then months. Nearly a year passed. The men played games, repaired the ship, made themselves useful. They seemed quite happy with their unexpected holiday. Odysseus helped Circe in the house and garden, and went to her bed every night. Aphrodite once asked me whether I had not been a little jealous of Circe but I denied it. I told her that, unlike her, I was not always worrying about who slept with whom. However, when spring came I thought there was a danger that Odysseus might forget his wife and home entirely, thus contradicting what the Fates (and Zeus) had ordained for him. So I went to Eurylochus in a dream and advised him to complain to Odysseus.

'It's all very well for you and this nymph,' he said, 'but we have wives and lovers whom we long to see. A year is quite long enough in this lonely island.'

Odysseus understood Eurylochus's objection and agreed they should return. Circe raised no opposition to their leaving, and she even supplied them with food and wine for their journey.

Now we come to the biggest mistake among the many that Odysseus made on this voyage, or at least the mistake with the worst consequences. He was not too far from Ithaca when his ship was driven off course by contrary winds. After several days of fruitless rowing they found themselves near an island which appeared inhabited as they could see green meadows and hear the lowing of cattle. Odysseus suspected that this might be the Island of the Sun which Circe had specifically warned him to avoid because it was where Helios kept his special herd of white cows that were tended by two of his daughters, and which he loved, and visited whenever he could. But Eurylochus and the others insisted on landing, saying they were exhausted with rowing and had to have time to recover, even if only for one night. Odysseus agreed, though he warned them on no account to touch any cows or sheep they might come across.

They fastened the ship to a rock and camped near the beach, preparing for their supper the remains of the food that Circe had given them for the voyage. The next morning a strong onshore wind made it impossible to leave the island, and this wind continued for several days during which the crew's hunger increased, although they did succeed in catching some fish. On the fourth day Odysseus left the others and climbed up a small hill so that he could pray to the gods undisturbed, and ask them for guidance. After his prayers, and feeling overcome by the midday heat, he fell asleep. But when he woke he was horrified to smell cooking. His men had seized two of the cows belonging to Helios, and were busy roasting the flesh on a fire.

For six days they feasted on the cows they had killed. Then on the seventh day the winds changed and they were able to set out on the open sea. But Helios had by now complained to Zeus who promised him that those who had eaten his sacred cattle would be punished. Zeus hurled one of his thunderbolts which struck and utterly destroyed the ship. All his men fell overboard and were washed away; Odysseus alone survived, due no doubt by the will of Zeus. He saw the mast and keel among the fragments of the ship floating in the water, and was able to lash them together and ride them. For many days he drifted, driven by the winds, until one morning he reached an island, home to the goddess Calypso, who saved him and cared for him.

CHAPTER 10: APHRODITE

AENEAS; FROM WAR TO DIDO

Not long after the death of my dear Paris came the destruction of Troy, the city closest to me in all the world. As everyone knows, the fall of Troy was due, not to the martial skills of the Greeks, but to a cunning and immoral scheme devised by Athena and her servant, Odysseus. It was the credulity of the Trojan leaders which permitted the famous wooden horse full of Greek soldiers to be dragged into the heart of the city and left there overnight. Those inside opened the city gates during the night, allowing the rest of the Greek army to enter, and to burn and murder at will.

I was now the only Olympian left who still supported the Trojans. Hera and Athena stood at the Scaean gate ushering in the Greek cohorts, and I could see brutal Ares wielding his sword against his former allies. From the heights of Mount Ida, Zeus was watching the sad destruction of a city he had always claimed to admire. He made no attempt to intervene. What could I do faced with such odds? All I could think of was to try and protect my son Aeneas and his family. He had put on his armour and rushed from his house when he first heard the tumult in the streets. He was searching for a like-minded group of Trojans whom he could join up with when he caught sight of Helen who was rushing to seek sanctuary in a temple, aware that she was hated by Greeks and Trojans alike. Aeneas ran after her, waving his sword. I could see he thought he might do the world a service by ridding it of the woman whom he believed to be the original cause of the war and its horrors. I stood in his path and addressed him.

'Oh my son, it is not the hated beauty of this Spartan woman that has ruined your city. It is the cruelty of the gods. Now please forget about Helen. You must escape from Troy as fast as you can, and I shall be by your side. Your destiny is to sail across the world to found a new city. But first go back home and collect your family – your wife Creusa, your father, and your little son Ascanius.'

Aeneas obeyed my command. At first Anchises refused to go with him, saying he would rather die at the hands of the Greeks than leave the city where he had spent most of his life. It was only when Creusa begged him not to abandon his own family that he finally agreed to go with them. Aeneas lifted his father onto his shoulders, took his son by the hand, and set off from his house with Creusa following closely behind. They made their way through the streets, and whenever they met other fleeing groups of Trojans, Aeneas told them to escape from the city by different routes and meet him at a certain spot – an old, abandoned temple in the woods. When Aeneas and his father reached the rendezvous they discovered that Creusa was no longer with them. Aeneas stormed and raged, and insisted on returning to Troy to look for her. But I knew what had happened to her. She had stopped, exhausted, and had then been attacked and murdered by a passing Greek soldier. I could not allow Aeneas to risk his own life in a fruitless search for his wife so I disguised myself, taking on the guise of a ghostly Creusa, and appeared on the path in front of him.

'My darling husband,' I said, 'why this wild grief? These things don't happen without cause. It is not the will of the gods that I should go with you when you leave this place.'

I prophesied that after many wanderings he would reach Italy and the river Tiber where he would found a new kingdom and marry a royal bride. Then I said goodbye, reminding him always to love and care for his little son.

Meanwhile a great crowd of those who had also escaped from the city had assembled at the old temple. Aeneas was amazed at how many there were: rich and poor, servants and masters. All accepted him as their leader, and it was decided to hide in the hills for a few days while messengers were sent to ports along the Phrygian coast asking for ships to be prepared for all those anxious to escape the Greek invasion. Eventually some twenty ships were gathered together, and when all was ready the fleet set sail early one morning with myself accompanying them. We voyaged across the sea to Thrace where it was expected that King Polymestor, an old ally of King Priam, would offer hospitality. The ships were anchored and food prepared for the evening meal when a most extraordinary incident took place. Aeneas was collecting leafy branches of myrtle wood to lay on a make-shift altar to the gods. He climbed a small mound not far from the beach and when he started tugging at the green shoots growing out of the earth he saw drops of blood on their roots. Then he heard a heart-rending groan emerge from the mound, and a voice spoke:

'Aeneas, why do you tear my poor flesh? Take pity on the man who is buried here. I am no stranger to you. It is Polydorus who speaks, and this is where I was struck down and buried.'

Aeneas knew, of course, that Polydorus, Priam's youngest son, had been sent to live with King Polymestor to protect him from the dangers of the war against Troy. As reward for looking after the boy, Priam had given Polymestor a large quantity of gold. Now the body buried under the mound explained to Aeneas what had happened. When the King of Thrace saw that the Greeks were going to win the war he rapidly changed sides. He kept the gold and had the boy murdered and buried in this remote spot.

Aeneas decided on revenge. He exhumed Polydorus's body and reburied it with religious rites. Then he told his Trojan followers to wait where they were until his return, and he sailed his own ship to a beach near the Thracian capital. He sent a message to King Polymestor saying how much he would like to meet him, and if possible his young sons as well. He was bringing gifts for them all. The meeting took place on the beach beside Aeneas's ship. Polymestor arrived hand in hand with his two sons, aged eight and ten, to be congratulated by his visitor:

'What handsome young men. You must be so proud of them. By the way, how is Prince Polydorus? Can we not meet him as well?'

Polymestor must have thought quickly. 'Unfortunately he is away hunting in the mountains. Several days' ride. What a shame! If only we had known you were coming.'

Now Aeneas had a small, sharp dagger in his hand which he dragged across the throat of the elder boy. A servant did the same to the younger. As their life blood poured onto the sand other Trojans grabbed Polymestor by the arms and held him in front of Aeneas who plunged his blade first into one eye socket and then into the other. Streams of Polymestor's blood mingled with the blood of his two sons.

'You murdered the last of Priam's line,' Aeneas screamed, 'and now the last thing you will ever see is the end of your own line.'

The butchery I witnessed on that beach deeply shocked me. This was not the calm and thoughtful Aeneas I had always known. I had promised to remain by his side in all his wanderings but now I felt I needed time to recover from what I had seen, so I left the Trojans to their own devices and retreated to my home in Olympia. Meanwhile Aeneas re-joined the rest of his ships.

During their travels, the Trojans were to suffer many setbacks while I was not there to protect them. At one point they sailed to Crete where they attempted to build a new city of their own, only to suffer from a devastating sickness which old Anchises took to be a warning that this was not the country the Fates had chosen for them. Later they anchored at the Strophades islands, home of the filthy harpies, half birds of prey and half women, who attacked them and polluted their food. Then they sailed northwards, along the coast of Epirus to Buthrotum where they made an unexpected and joyful encounter. The ruler of this city turned out to be a Trojan prince named Helenus, one of Priam's many sons. He was now married to Andromache, widow of the great Hector. Helenus and Andromache treated their fellow countrymen with great hospitality, lavishing on them many precious gifts, and Helenus, who had the gift of prophesy, gave them valuable advice before they left Buthrotum. He told them that if they were to fulfil their destiny they must first travel southwards back to Sicily and then, having rounded that island, sail north along the western coast of Italy until they reached the Tiber River. On no account should they try to land on the eastern side of Italy, although of course it seemed the obvious route for them, because many Greeks had settled along that coast. Nor should they try to shorten their journey by crossing the Strait of Messina which separated Sicily from Italy. That way led to Scylla and Charybdis, two monsters that preyed on passing seamen.

The Trojans sailed southwards from Buthrotum and followed the advice they had been given. Having reached Sicily they decided to stay for the night at a beach on the east coast of the island, not far from Mount Etna. This was the domain of the Cyclopes, and I now realised that Helenus, for all his gift of prophesy, had never mentioned the threat that these one-eyed cannibal giants posed to humans. Therefore I decided to return, and if possible save them from this danger. I knew that not long before the Trojans arrived, Odysseus and his men had come here and had been imprisoned in a cave by a Cyclops named Polyphemus. Some of them had been killed and eaten, and the rest were very lucky to escape with their lives. So I disguised myself as a member of Odysseus's crew who had run in the wrong direction after escaping from Polyphemus, and who had been hiding alone in the forest while the rest escaped by ship. I gave myself a straggling beard and bloodshot eyes. My body was filthy and I wore tattered rags pinned together with thorns. I came out of the woods and approached the Trojans with my hands held out in supplication. I explained who I was and how we had escaped from Polyphemus by making him drunk and then, when he had fallen into a deep sleep, boring into his only eye with a sharpened stick. I told how I had survived for two months, hiding from the Cyclopes as they tended their sheep on the slopes of the mountain. My only food had been berries and herbs from the forest. Then I warned the Trojans to escape now, before the Cyclopes became aware of their presence, and I begged them to take me with them, which they agreed to do. True, I was Greek and therefore their enemy, but all felt I had suffered enough. Even while we were speaking they caught sight of Polyphemus – a terrifying sight with his enormous bulk and his forehead still caked with blood. He was stumbling along, using a willow stick to guide his footsteps. They watched as he entered the sea to bathe his empty eye socket. Then he somehow became aware of our presence and screamed out to his neighbours who came running down the mountain towards us. The Trojans rushed to man their ship and to row away from this unspeakable land – and I went with them.

We continued our journey as Helenus had advised, but at Drepanum on the north-west corner of Sicily there occurred a sad, though not unexpected, event. Aeneas's old father Anchises died. The rough seas, lack of sleep and irregular meals had taken their toll. We buried him with all honours and went on our way. But now we were struck by a sudden storm worse than any we had ever experienced. Of course Hera was behind it. I realised she had no intention of ever giving up her ruthless pursuit of these pathetic fugitives from Troy. She was someone who never forgave nor forgot a presumed injury or insult, and, even after all these years, she was still angry about losing that contest, and the slight to her beauty when I won it. Now she was also aware of the prediction of the Fates that one day the descendants of Aeneas would create a great empire which would overthrow Carthage, the city she loved best in the world. She had gone to Aeolus, keeper of the winds, and begged him to release his most brutal storm winds from the cavern where they were held prisoner. She promised him the loveliest of her nymphs in marriage if he could succeed in sinking the Trojan fleet, and he agreed.

In the face of this terrible storm there was little to be done. The sky went black and powerful winds drove the ships in every direction while mountainous waves crashed over them, destroying masts and rudders and sweeping men overboard. The fleet was widely scattered and many Trojans drowned when their ships were driven onto reefs or rocky shores. Of the original twenty that had left Troy, only seven ships survived the storm. Luckily Poseidon, from his palace in the depths of the ocean, came up to see what was happening. He was not pleased and summoned the winds to him.

'How dare you raise these great waves without my divine authority? Back to your cavern, and remind Aeolus that it is I, not he, who rules over the oceans.'

Poseidon calmed the sea, allowing Aeneas to lead those ships that had survived the storm to the nearest land, which happened to be the Libyan shore.

When I saw what had been done to the Trojan ships, I came to Zeus, my eyes full of tears.

'What great harm has Aeneas ever done you that you punish him so brutally?' I blurted out. 'You promised me he would lead his people to Italy, and there found a new kingdom. Now Aeolus has released his terrible winds and the Trojan fleet is scattered in all directions. Their ships have been wrecked, and many Trojans drowned. Oh Father, it seems you have suddenly changed your mind about my beloved son. Has he not suffered enough for you?'

Father Zeus looked at me with his usual smile. 'Spare yourself these fears, my lady from Cythera. The destiny of your son is fixed and cannot change. I never ordered my servant Aeolus to release those winds, and I will question him and find out why he did.'

'I do not think you need look very far, father,' I replied. 'I believe you know that there is one who is not my friend, and who hates all the Trojans. It seems it is not enough for her that the city of Troy has been razed to the ground.'

Zeus merely shrugged his shoulders.

After this rather unsatisfactory interview I flew down to the Libyan coast where Aeneas had beached his badly damaged ship. The crew were lying about on the sand trying to recover from the storm and eating what few provisions they had left. The other Trojan ships that had survived the storms were drawn up on another beach not far away. Then I saw Aeneas with one companion leave the rest of his crew in order to explore what was to them a totally unknown countryside. They took a path up the hill, on the lookout for dangerous beasts or humans – if there were any humans. I felt the time had come to give some guidance to my son so I took on the appearance of a local girl out hunting. I wore a rough woollen dress and purple boots with a high ankle binding. My unbound hair streamed in the wind. I carried a light bow and had a quiver tied to my waist.

'Hello there, soldiers,' I called out. 'Do you happen to have seen my two brothers? They were on this path a few minutes ago.'

We fell into conversation and I made them aware of the city named Carthage which was then in process of construction not far from where we stood. I also told them about its queen, Dido, who had fled from Tyre, a city far to the east, after her husband, Sychaeus, had been murdered by her own brother. In a dream Hera, pretending to be her dead husband, had warned Dido to flee, and to take with her some followers and also the treasure that Sychaeus had saved up. Now here she was in Libya, organising the building of this new city. I told them that if they climbed to the top of the hill they could see Carthage, and within its half-built walls a royal palace, and also a huge temple dedicated to Hera, who was Dido's patron goddess. In reply, Aeneas recounted to me the story of Troy and how he had come to be on the island, which of course I already knew. I could tell that Aeneas had his suspicions about who I really was, but I chose to say nothing.

CHAPTER 11: ATHENA & APHRODITE

A RECONCILIATION

Scene: Athena's palace at Olympia. Aphrodite enters and sits down.

Athena: Oh Aphrodite, so glad to have caught you. I haven't really seen you since the war ended. Can we have a quick word? First, I want to apologise for the way Diomedes threw his spear at you when you were just trying to save your son. It was inexcusable to treat a goddess in the way he did. I do hope that cut on your arm didn't hurt too much.

Aphrodite: Well, yes it did hurt – but of course it healed quite quickly. Was there anything else you wanted to say to me?

Athena: I know you've been very busy helping Aeneas, which is why I haven't seen you. How is that going, by the way?

Aphrodite: As you've probably heard, Hera has been sending storm winds to try and stop Aeneas's fleet getting to Italy – and sink as many of their ships as possible. She still hates all Trojans – even though Troy itself has long since been burnt to ashes.

Athena: Yes, she never forgets a grudge, does she. Actually,

I'm quite pleased I'm no longer at her beck and call as I was during the war. I have my own project now – which is looking after Odysseus. And he certainly needs looking after. Left to himself he makes all kinds of stupid mistakes.

Aphrodite: To get back to Aeneas – he's actually been very lucky. Poseidon found out that Hera was telling the winds what to do and he got very angry because he thought it was none of her business, so he locked them all back in their cave. And when the storms stopped, Aeneas and his Trojans were able to beach their ships peacefully on a stretch of coastline near Carthage.

Athena: Aeneas is so lucky to have Poseidon on his side. It's just the opposite with Odysseus. Ever since he blinded Poseidon's son, Polyphemus, Odysseus has been threatened by storms sent by Poseidon. It's true that when Odysseus was living on Circe's island, he was relatively safe. But as soon as Circe let him go he was again at the mercy of angry gods.

Aphrodite: Tell me more about Circe. I met her when she was a young nymph but haven't seen her since her father, Helios, made her go and live on that island all by herself.

Athena: She's a powerful witch now. You heard how she treated Odysseus's crew.

Aphrodite: Yes. Turned them into pigs. But then he made love to her and she turned them back again. I gather Odysseus lived with her for over a year and had two sons by her. Were you jealous?

Athena: Jealousy is hardly my thing.

Aphrodite: Not even a little bit? I believe she's very beautiful.

Athena: Not even a little bit. I told you about my oath.

Anyway, why would I be jealous of Odysseus? His legs are far too short.

Aphrodite: Perhaps you prefer your own sex? I've heard rumours about you when you were young – you and that water nymph. What was her name? Oh yes, Pallas.

Athena: Well, I've heard rumours about you and Hera. When you helped her try on your magic corset. And then – I was meaning to ask you – what about Poseidon? Didn't you once make love to him?

Aphrodite: That was so long ago I can hardly remember. He's had dozens of lovers since then – male and female.

Athena: More lovers than you? (*A pause.*) Come and sit beside me. *(Both move to the sofa. Athena puts her arm round Aphrodite.)*

Aphrodite: You know you do look so attractive – without your helmet and armour.

Athena: Not quite as attractive as you, darling. At least that's what Paris thought in that famous contest.

Aphrodite: You know perfectly well that was only because I promised him Helen.

Athena: No, you won because you really are the most beautiful being in the whole world.

Aphrodite: If I forgive you for what you did to me in the war, will you forgive me for winning that contest?

Athena: Of course I will. And now we can be real friends. *(Tears came into Aphrodite's eyes as Athena puts her arm round her and gives her a long kiss.)*

CHAPTER 12: HERA

HERA AND DIDO

I have known Dido since she was a young girl in the city of Tyre. She and her father were my worshippers. When she was sixteen her father gave her in marriage to the rich Phoenician, Sychaeus, who treated her well and whom she came to love deeply. But Dido's brother, Pygmalion, who inherited Tyre after her father died, was a godless criminal, and in his lust for gold he dragged Sychaeus away when he was praying at my altar and stabbed him to death. No one had any idea who the murderer was until I appeared to Dido one night in the likeness of Sychaeus with blood streaming from his wounds. I revealed to her the horror of her brother's crime, and advised her to escape from Tyre with all speed. I showed her the place where Sychaeus had buried his gold. She must dig up the treasure, and enlist some like-minded followers – those who hated or feared Pygmalion. Then find suitable ships ready for sea and leave Tyre with all speed before Pygmalion realised what was going on.

Now, with my help, Dido and her subjects came to the

Libyan coast to found a new city called Carthage in a place where before there was only pasture and rough ground. To achieve this she first had to impress the local chieftains who between them owned all the land. She did this partly by her own charm and winning personality and partly by a clever trick. The trick came after they had jokingly agreed to give her as much land as could be covered by an ox hide. She got a skilful seamstress to cut the ox hide into one long and very thin strip which, when spread out, covered far more land than the chieftains had bargained for. They were so impressed by her cleverness that in the end they gave her even more land. Then they sent her their best carpenters and builders to help the fugitives from Tyre create their new city. Dido now showed herself to be a woman of exceptional gifts and naturally the Tyrians whom she had brought with her welcomed her authority. She used to get up early every morning to supervise the work or to discuss new laws and regulations for the citizens. The largest and most beautiful building in the city – apart from the royal palace – is my temple, where prayers and sacrifices are offered to me daily. The queen continues to worship and honour me, as she has done all her life, and I will continue to look after her and protect her from harm.

As I watched the creation of Dido's Carthage it became my determination that one day this city would exceed all other cities in its fame and power. It would triumph over its enemies, win every contest, and create an empire such as the world had never seen. I must admit here that part of this ambition of mine – the major part perhaps – came from my rivalry with my own husband. Zeus wanted Aeneas to found a new city called Rome which would one day conquer Carthage and become the capital of an empire. Zeus, of course, is King of the gods and said to be all-powerful. But I am Hera, Queen of the gods. I possess a will of my own and at that time, I intended to exert it.

Dido never forgot her old life in Tyre, and the ghastly murder of the husband she had loved so dearly. She always swore he would never be replaced in her heart by another. Nevertheless, I was worried about her position as a female ruler surrounded by kings and chieftains, some of whom would have loved to make her an offer of marriage. How long could she maintain her independence? Might Carthage fall into the hands of a godless African dynasty? Then I saw the remainder of the Trojan fleet beached on the Libyan shore close to Carthage, and an idea came to me – to promote a marriage between Queen Dido and the Trojan leader. After all, Aeneas was also a fugitive from his own country. If Dido took pity on him and saved him and his followers from the stormy seas, then he would owe his good fortune and even his life to her. With divine assistance, perhaps a romantic affair and eventually a marriage could be arranged. Aeneas, of course, would have to forget about his so-called destiny in Italy. My arrogant husband might be forced to re-think his plans.

At the banquet given by Dido in her palace the evening after the day the Trojans arrived in Carthage, Aeneas recounted to all the guests stories of his adventures. It was then that Aphrodite exercised her powers. She ordered her servant, Eros, to assume the likeness of Ascanius, the young son of Aeneas (the real Ascanius having been spirited away for the evening to Aphrodite's shrine in Cythera). Then, when Dido was nursing the little boy that she thought was Ascanius, Eros shot a tiny magic arrow into the Queen's heart, which conveyed an all-consuming love for Aeneas. When the banquet was over and all the guests had left I overheard Dido talking to her sister.

'Oh Anna, I am in such a quandary. This stranger who has come into our house – you heard him tell how cruelly he has been hounded by the Fates. And yet he has survived. What a hero he is! And how good-looking! This is the only man who has stirred my feelings since my husband's cruel death. But I made a sacred vow that no other man will ever supplant my love for Sichaeus. What am I to do?'

Anna embraced her, and replied, 'My darling sister, are you going to waste away your entire life in mourning what happened in the past? Will you never experience the joys of love and the delights of children? This stranger is worthy of you. To what pinnacle of glory would Carthage be raised if you were to marry such a man? It was surely by favour of the gods that Aeneas and his Trojans landed here, and I believe it was for you.'

Such words replaced Dido's guilt with hope. Now her passion was so powerful that she gave up all her daily duties as queen, and her labours in planning her new city. She spent as much time as she could with Aeneas, asking him questions about his life, or driving round the city with him to show him off to the citizens. Since the goddess of love had chosen to interfere so dramatically in Dido's life I thought it high time I recruited her to my cause. I paid her a visit in her palace at Olympus.

'Aphrodite,' I said. 'I know we have had our arguments in the past, but don't you think that now is the time we should work together? Our interests coincide – you for Aeneas and I for Dido.'

'Our arguments in the past?' she retorted angrily. 'Do you mean your efforts to completely destroy the great city of Troy, and your mad determination to drown the pathetic remnant of the Trojan race who managed to escape, including my own dearest son?'

I knew this would be a difficult interview but I did my best to conciliate her.

'Aphrodite, I admit all your charges. I did support the Greeks against the Trojans, and I did persuade Aeolus to unleash his storm winds against Aeneas's fleet. But now that the Trojans are here in Carthage the situation has changed. I know you find it difficult to trust me, but will you at least listen to my suggestion. I want to arrange a marriage between Dido and Aeneas, and I think that is also what you want.'

'Zeus would never allow such a marriage,' she said. 'You know perfectly well that he expects Aeneas to go to Italy and found a new kingdom there.'

'My husband may be King of the gods,' I replied, 'but he does not always get what he wants. And I think that if he tried to separate a loving married couple he would face the opposition of all the other gods.'

Aphrodite thought for a minute and then agreed to hear my plan.

'Listen,' I told her, 'Aeneas and Dido are preparing to go hunting together in the forest tomorrow. When the beaters are scurrying about and setting up their nets I shall bring about a storm of rain, and shake the sky with thunder. The two of them will take shelter in the same cave after all their companions have run away into the darkness. There, if you are with me in this, they will fall into each other's arms. After they have made love I shall join them together in lasting marriage, and make her his and him hers. This will be their wedding, and even my husband would hesitate to break the bonds of such a sacred union.'

I knew of course that the goddess of love would be unable to resist the idea of her son and Queen Dido making love, and I was right. We agreed on what to do. I would bring about the storm and she would sort out a bed for them in the cave.

The following day everything went according to my plan. It was a beautiful morning. Numerous servants carried up food and drink from the palace kitchens to a glade high in the woods that had been chosen as a picnic site. All the Trojans and a crowd of Dido's citizens followed, some to hunt, others merely to enjoy a holiday with their queen. Suddenly the weather changed dramatically. Black clouds gathered, and flashes of lightning lit up the sky. Then it started to rain and everyone rushed to whatever cover they could find. Dido seized Aeneas by the hand.

'I know a cave not far from here,' she told him. 'If we hurry we might just make it before we get completely soaked.'

She was wrong – they were sopping wet by the time they reached the mouth of the cave. Inside was a long flat stone on which straw had been piled, and there were pillows and a couple of woollen blankets.

'Look what I've found,' exclaimed Aeneas.

'Some hunter or shepherd must have spent the night here,' said Dido.

Aeneas laughed: 'Shall we try it out?'

He picked Dido up and carried her to the stone. They undressed each other, lay down, and started to make love while Aphrodite and I watched. When they had finished I crept up and whispered in Dido's ear. I told her that now they were married and must never be parted. Their marriage had been witnessed by the gods.

When Dido and Aeneas got back to the picnic site the storm was over. Everyone was wondering where they were. She made a speech to the crowd:

116

'Can I have your attention please. This is a great day for me and for Carthage. Lord Aeneas, who was sent to our city by the favour of the gods, has just become my husband, and today is our wedding day.'

She went on to ask them to raise their goblets to Hera, Queen of the gods, who had arranged the marriage. Then she invited them all to a feast in the palace that evening. My ambition had succeeded, and I assumed that Aeneas and Dido would now share the throne of Carthage as king and queen.

Unfortunately, from this point things started to go very wrong. Rumours had reached Zeus that Aeneas appeared to be shirking the destiny that had been planned for him. When, my husband asked himself, would the Trojans say goodbye to Carthage and set sail for Italy? What did Aeneas think he was doing spending his time helping Queen Dido build a city on the Libyan coast? And then it was rumoured he had actually married her. How could that be? Zeus knew of my affection for Dido and guessed that I had a hand in it. He summoned Hermes and bade him glide down to the Trojan leader who was lingering in Carthage without a thought for his destiny in Italy.

'Ask him,' said Zeus, 'what he has in mind. What does he hope to achieve by dallying in a strange land? Tell him that he must sail immediately.'

Hermes did as Zeus ordered. His words struck Aeneas with horror. Now he longed to be away from this city he had found so sweet. He gave orders to his crew to fit out the fleet and prepare to leave, but not to tell anyone. However, the queen soon heard about what was being planned.

She went to Aeneas and cried, 'You traitor, did you think you could slip away from my land and say nothing? Does

117

our marriage and our love have no claim on you at all?'

He struggled to reply. He told her of the visit from Hermes, and pleaded with her: 'It is not by my own will that I must search for Italy, but by the command of Zeus.'

But his pleas fell on deaf ears. Dido screamed at him in her anger and her pain until she fainted, falling to the ground, and had to be carried to her bed in the palace.

The whole situation was made worse because the goddess of love now chose once again to interfere. She had spoken to Elissa, the young girl whom Aeneas had asked to look after his son, Ascanius. Aphrodite imbued Elissa with a powerful love for Aeneas, and in the middle of the night woke her up and, holding her hand, led her to his bedroom. But a guard sitting at the end of the corridor had seen her going into his bedroom and reported this to Dido who then summoned Elissa to her room. I listened to what was said. Dido started by screaming and cursing, telling Elissa she must leave the palace that day. She never wanted to see her again. However, after both women had sat on the bed for some time, speechless and sobbing, Dido changed her mind. It was Aeneas's – fault. Not Elissa's..

That night the Trojan ships left their moorings and sailed away from the Libyan coast. Dido, after a sleepless night, knew what had to be done. She gave orders that a pyre of wood be erected in the inner courtyard of the palace. On it, she placed all the belongings that Aeneas had left behind, including his armour, his clothing, the gifts she had given him, and on top of it all, the bed in which they had spent so many loving hours. When her sister asked her why, Dido explained that it was to help her erase him from her memory. While the pyre was being laid Dido hid in her room to offer up to me a secret prayer: that the Trojans would fail in their quest to found a new kingdom in Italy, that Aeneas would die, killed by his enemies, that his body would remain unburied. I heard her prayer.

When she was ready, Dido entered the courtyard holding a torch. She lit the bottom of the pyre and then climbed up a ladder to reach the bed. She was holding a sword that had once belonged to Aeneas, and which she told her attendants they had forgotten to add to the pyre. I knew what she was going to do but I was powerless to prevent it. She stood on the bed, held the sword with its point over her heart, and then fell onto it. The witnesses standing round the pyre screamed and Anna rushed into the courtyard and climbed the ladder. She held her dying sister to her breast, sobbing as she dried the dark blood with her own breast.

A figure was hovering in the air above the pyre. It was Aphrodite. She had seen the smoke rising and had flown over from Aeneas's ship.

'This is all your doing, you so-called goddess of love,' I shouted at her. 'Goddess of pain, more likely. Your meddling has resulted in the death of this virtuous queen. Aren't you ashamed of yourself?'

She made no reply and flew back to the Trojan ships. I reminded myself never again to try and cooperate with Aphrodite.

CHAPTER 13: APHRODITE

APHRODITE AND DIDO

I saw Aeneas and his friend Achates climb the hill and view the new city. As they were admiring it they became aware that a delegation of their companions from the other Trojan ships had arrived at the city walls and were about to meet Dido and her courtiers who were standing in front of the royal palace. The two of them therefore rushed down the hill to join their compatriots. I was worried that this collection of ragged strangers might receive a hostile reception, but my fears proved groundless. After they had explained who they were, Dido welcomed them to Carthage, promising that arrangements would be made for their living quarters for as long as they wanted to stay, and that workmen and materials would be made available for the repair of their damaged ships. She invited all the Trojans to a banquet at her palace the following evening. Yet, in spite of this apparently favourable reception, I was still worried about the ultimate fate of all these foreigners in this unknown land. I knew that Dido worshipped Hera,

Queen of the gods, and that Hera saw all Trojans as enemies. I knew, too, that it had been Hera who had persuaded Aeolus to release the winds that had wrecked so many of their ships.

Aeneas and some other Trojan leaders were invited to stay in the palace, and the rest were dispersed to households around the town. Aeneas then requested that his son, who had remained with the ships, be brought to join him. Ascanius was six years old, a lively child and the apple of his father's eye. But I had other plans. First I put Ascanius into a deep sleep and transported him to my sacred shrine on the heights of Cythera. Then I called my own son, Eros, god of love, who was not much older than Ascanius, to use his magic powers and make himself take on the appearance of Aeneas's son for just one night. Between us, we worked out what we would do. Eros was to appear when the banquet at the palace was nearly over and when Dido took him onto her lap – which she was sure to do – he had to inject her with a passionate love for Aeneas. It seemed to me – at least at that time – that this would be the most obvious and successful cause of action.

The plan worked. The banquet was an impressive affair that showed what the palace kitchens could achieve, even at such short notice. It lasted well into the night until, after speeches from Dido and Aeneas, the guests, replete with food and slightly drunk, started to quit the banqueting hall. Long before this, "Ascanius" – or rather Eros – had been put to bed in a nearby chamber by his newly appointed nursemaid, a young girl called Elissa, who undertook to sit on a stool near his bed and watch over him. Now it was my turn. I crept into their bedroom, sent Elissa into a brief sleep and then alerted Eros who, as we had planned, came prancing into the hall waving his hands in the air.

'Come here, darling, and sit with me,' called out Dido. Meanwhile, I had entered the hall invisibly and hidden one of Eros's short arrows under the dinner table near Dido's feet. Now Elissa rushed into the hall in pursuit of her charge.

'I can't understand how he found his way here,' she cried. 'I must have dozed off. I'm so sorry.'

'Think nothing of it,' said Aeneas. 'He's fairly uncontrollable.'

Dido held out her hands to the little boy, and he dived under the table and came up beside her, to be lifted onto her lap and cuddled. He returned her kisses with enthusiasm but at the same time, without her noticing, pricked her with his arrow on the cleavage between her breasts.

'Let me take him, madam,' said Elissa. She left carrying Eros, the remaining guests also left and so did I, but Dido was leaning back in her chair, a contented smile on her face. The arrow had disappeared.

Over the next few weeks Dido was on fire with love. She spent as much time with Aeneas as she possibly could, failing to supervise the building of Carthage and her other royal duties. Sometimes she took him for long rides in her carriage, and often I saw them sitting close together whispering to each other, either in the courtyard of the palace or after a meal when the other guests had departed. Lacking her presence and authority, the half-built walls and towers of the city now became neglected. Rumours started concerning the queen and this stranger with whom she was so clearly obsessed. Hera, of course, heard the rumours and noticed how Dido had changed. She guessed that I was responsible, and one day she came to my hall in Olympus to confront me.

'I know this infatuation of Dido's is your doing, and I

understand why you did it,' she said. 'You wanted to protect your son Aeneas in case the people of Carthage turned against these strangers from the sea. But can't you see that the rumours now flying around about Queen Dido are making Aeneas and his Trojans even more unpopular?'

I had to admit that she had a point, and asked her what she thought should be done.

'You and I are both involved here,' she said. 'You with Aeneas and I with Dido. Can we not work together? I know we have not always been friends, but now don't you think it's time to cooperate?'

She said we should arrange a marriage between the two, and then Dido's subjects and the Trojans would live together in peace forever. Aeneas and Dido could share the royal authority as king and queen, and with our divine help Carthage might become the richest and most powerful city in the world. I asked how this marriage might be brought about, especially as we knew that her husband, Zeus, had quite another destiny in view for Aeneas. If I were willing to join with her, she said, my task would be to prepare a bed for them in a cave she would show me, where they might make love. I was sceptical about Hera's proposal. I thought it was devised just to please Dido who throughout her life had worshipped the Queen of the gods, and who was just building a vast and beautiful temple dedicated to her. I also saw this plan as just another event in the long and bitter rivalry between Hera and her husband. I knew she was up for anything which might thwart one of Zeus's pet projects – in this case, the foundation of Rome by Aeneas. And, finally, I doubted whether it would succeed. Who could possibly consider a secret act of lovemaking in a cave the equivalent of a legal marriage? Nor could it stop Aeneas from one day sailing away from Carthage to fulfil his destiny. In spite of all these objections I decided it might be better to retain Hera's goodwill for the time being, so I agreed to what she was proposing.

Everything went as we had decided. The queen, along with Aeneas and his followers and large numbers from the city, walked or rode to a clearing in the forest between two rocky hills. Here, the servants were just setting out a magnificent picnic when black storm clouds obscured the sun and the rumble of thunder was heard. Rain started to pour down and the crowd scattered, searching for shelter. Dido took Aeneas by the hand.

'Come with me, my dear,' she said. 'I know a cave not far from here where we can shelter.' She led him to a small opening halfway up the rocky hillside. When they squeezed through they found themselves in a large chamber which seemed much brighter than it should have been. I followed them – though unseen by my guests. I was aware that Hera was there waiting for us. Deep inside the cave Aeneas came across a flat rock with a covering of straw, lamb's wool and blankets. Yes, I had prepared the way for them, and now I inserted into Dido's mind what we had planned for her:

'He's my son,' I told her. 'Take him as your husband and let him lead you to your marriage bed. Here, just behind you, there's a hollow in the rock which I have prepared for you. You can lie here together, and when you rise from this bed, you will be husband and wife. I have told you so and it's true.'

Dido hardly needed my prompting. After a lingering embrace the two of them stripped off their wet clothes, collapsed together onto the rock, and began the kissing, touching and stroking that always comes before the act of making love. After it was all over I saw Hera creep to Dido's side and whisper to her,

124

'Now your dream has come true. When you rise from this couch you and Aeneas will be married and can never be parted.'

The storm had long subsided when Dido and Aeneas returned to the hunt picnic.

'Listen to me please, my people,' the queen called out, 'I have something to announce. Lord Aeneas, who was sent to Carthage by the favour of the gods, has just become my husband. Divine Hera and Aphrodite have witnessed our marriage. I ask you all to raise your goblets to us, to our future, and to the goddesses who have made this union possible.'

Everyone clapped and hastened to congratulate Dido, but I could see that some were wondering how such a marriage could possibly have taken place – in such secrecy, and without a priest. It was at this point that I reassessed the situation that I had myself partly brought about. I was mainly concerned that Aeneas, swept up in this new love, might now decide to stay in Carthage, abandoning his destiny and going against the will of Almighty Zeus. The marriage – such as it was – was in danger of upsetting my plans! It occurred to me that one way to dissolve, or at least weaken, this so-called marriage might be to demonstrate to Dido that her new 'husband' was not to be trusted when it came to other women. So, in the weeks ahead, while the couple enjoyed each other's company during the day and shared the same bed at night, I pondered how to bring this about. I noticed that when he was not out with Dido Aeneas seemed to spend time sitting in the courtyard of the palace watching his son, Ascanius at play. One day I realised, from the glances he kept giving her, that this was at least partly because he enjoyed chatting to Elissa, the little boy's attractive young nursemaid with her long brown hair and blue eyes. I decided to do a little research.

One evening, when Ascanius had been put to bed, I came across Elissa sitting by herself on a bench facing the pond in the middle of the courtyard. Assuming the appearance of one of the older Trojan women who had come to Carthage with Aeneas, I sat down beside her and started a conversation.

'I heard you were a seamstress making clothes for Dido until recently,' I said. 'What's it like having to be a nursemaid instead?'

This got her going and she told me all about herself. How she had run away from home when she was only fourteen because her father was planning to marry her off to a neighbour she hated, how she had been found hiding near the palace by a guard and taken to the queen, how Dido had been so kind to her:

She asked me my name, and when I told her 'Elissa' she said that was strange because it was also her real name, except that now people always called her Dido.

'Fate must have intended us to meet each other,' Dido had told her.

She then asked if Elissa could sew, and when she said she had sewn clothes for her little sisters and brothers, she gave her a job in the sewing workshop, and also a room in the palace, sharing with two other girls.

After two years as a seamstress Elissa had been honoured when Dido suggested she might leave the sewing room and look after Ascanius instead. So then I asked Elissa about Ascanius. She said he was very sweet but quite difficult to control. The other day, for instance, he had suddenly jumped into the pond and got completely soaked. He managed to grab a fish and started waving it about in the air, calling it Odysseus. Just then Aeneas happened to arrive and Elissa had felt sure he would tell her off for not watching Ascanius properly, but he said it was not at all her fault. Aeneas, she said, was always really charming and polite to her.

Later, a rumour started to go round the palace that the Trojans were preparing their ships to sail away from Carthage. I heard it was because Zeus had sent down his messenger, Hermes, to tell Aeneas it was time for him to leave. That night I visited Elissa when she was asleep, and I made her dream about Aeneas – about how handsome he was, and what it would be like to be kissed by him and lie in his arms. The following evening Aeneas was again in the courtyard watching Ascanius play and chatting to Elissa. He told her the rumour was true. Very soon he and all the Trojans would be leaving, and how much he would miss her when they did.

In the middle of that night Elissa got out of her bed quietly so as not to wake the other girls and crept down the long corridor to Aeneas' room. I went with her and held her hand, though no mortal could see me. I noticed that one of the palace guards was sitting at the end of the corridor apparently drowsing and I wondered whether he might have seen Elissa. She went into Aeneas's bedroom, woke him with a kiss, and then, climbing into bed beside him, whispered that she had come to say goodbye. At first he seemed shocked by her presence and leapt out of the bed, but when she started to cry he hugged her, and soon they were both naked and wrapped in each other's arms. The goddess of love had triumphed again!

Before dawn Elissa was back in her own bed. The girls she shared her room with had noticed her absence and asked her where she had been, but she wouldn't say. They told her all the Trojans had been ordered down to the ships and were planning to sail away on the next tide. Later that day Dido sent for Elissa, and I followed, invisibly, to hear what was said. When she first went into Dido's bedroom, the queen was looking out of the window with her back to her. Then she suddenly turned round and we could see her eyes were red with crying. There was a pause while she stared at Elissa and then she started shouting:

'I know what you did last night. you randy little whore! My husband in bed with my servant! It's disgusting. You have betrayed me, my trust in you, my love for you. Go away. I hate you. Leave my palace. I never want to have to look at you again.'

Dido sat down on the bed shaking, her face in her hands. There was a much longer pause, both of them in tears. Then, suddenly, a change of mood. Dido held out her hand to Elissa and made her sit beside her.

'Oh, Elissa, I'm so sorry. It's not your fault. I'm being cruel. I forgive you. I don't want you to go away. Its him, my so-called husband. He has betrayed us both. That's what he's like, totally selfish. He left without saying a word to me. And last night you only did what I also once did, using the word marriage to cover my guilt. You persuaded him to make love to you but why should you be punished when I too have acted like a love-sick fool?'

Meanwhile, down at the harbour, Aeneas had ordered his men to let out the sails of their ships and undo the mooring cables, and the rowers to sit on their benches. And I, his mother, prepared myself to accompany the Trojan ships as they crossed the seas towards the land of their destiny. When we had sailed a mile or two from Carthage, looking back we saw a thin column of smoke rising from the royal palace. I knew what this must mean, and I left the ship and flew back across the water. Approaching the palace I heard a terrible wailing, and saw flames licking a great pile of wood in the centre of the courtyard. And on top of the pile was the dying body of Queen Dido who had just thrown herself onto a sword, the point of which was sticking out of her back. Elissa, as well as Dido's sister, Anna, were bending over the body, trying in vain to pull the sword from under Dido's breast. And now I saw, hovering above the dying body, Hera, the patron goddess of Carthage. When she saw me she started shouting, accusing me of causing Dido's death. I could have contradicted her, pointing out her own responsibility for the tragedy, but I chose not to. My first duty was to protect my son, so I left Carthage, never to return.

CHAPTER 14: ATHENA

ODYSSEUS AND NAUSICAA

After the war I collaborated with Poseidon to prevent the Greeks reaching their homes. We succeeded in drowning Ajax who was the Greek leader I hated most because he had desecrated my temple in Troy by raping Cassandra when she sought sanctuary there. But I never really got on with Poseidon. I started to change my mind regarding the Greeks, especially about Odysseus whom Poseidon continued to harass. Much of my old sympathy for Odysseus returned when I saw the last ship in his fleet destroyed and himself nearly drowned by storms sent by Poseidon. Then Odysseus was cast up on Ogygia, the island belonging to the nymph Calypso, and he became virtually her prisoner. She was certainly kind to the exhausted stranger she found lying on her beach. She nursed him and gave him everything he needed, except his freedom. She even gave him a share in her bed, which he didn't need and soon became tired of. I saw him become sadder and more deeply depressed as time passed with no hope of escape.

Every day he used to sit on a cliff top staring out to sea, searching for the ship that never came.

At this stage I decided to help Odysseus again, just as I had so often done in the past. I wanted the old Odysseus back – the one who was full of tricks and lies, who never took himself too seriously and was seldom boring, unlike most of the so-called heroes. The problem was that if I got him off Calypso's island he would be back at sea, and the seas were controlled by Poseidon who had never forgiven him for blinding his son Polyphemus. – much like Hera, Poseidon never forgot old grievances. He knew Odysseus was destined to return to his home in Ithaca, but he also knew how to delay this return indefinitely – and humans are only mortal. I didn't want to get into a quarrel with Poseidon so I had to wait until he went on one of his trips, which he occasionally did. One day I heard he was off to visit the Ethiopians and was likely to stay there some time. They lived on the other side of the world, and were great favourites of his. I seized my chance and went to see Zeus to remind him of his promise that Odysseus would one day return to Ithaca.

At a meeting of the gods on Olympus I put the question to Zeus as to whether or not he had forgotten his pledge, and he assured me he had not. When I explained the situation, Zeus agreed it was high time something was done. He ordered his messenger Hermes to go down to Ogygia and tell Calypso she must let her prisoner go. Hermes told me later how angry she had been when he passed her the message:

'You cruel, jealous gods!' she cried. 'You resent it whenever any goddess takes a mortal to sleep with as a lover in her bed.'

She told Hermes everything she had done for Odysseus

since he was washed up half dead on her beach:

'This was a man I saved. I cared for him and loved him, and I asked him to be my husband.'

According to her she had even offered him immortality if he agreed to stay with her, though how she had the power to do that I cannot imagine, since she was really only a nymph, although she described herself as a goddess. Either way, he had refused her offers and kept talking about Ithaca and whether his darling wife was still alive.

'Nevertheless,' she eventually conceded, 'I suppose, since Zeus has ordered it, I'd better obey.'

'Yes, you had,' Hermes replied, 'and don't hang around or Zeus will be very angry.'

Then he flew back to Olympus.

Calypso did as she had promised. She went to find Odysseus and explained Zeus's command that he must leave her island. She told him that as she did not possess a boat he would have to use his skills to make himself a raft. At first he didn't believe her story.

'Goddess,' he said, 'you have some new scheme in mind. How can I cross this vast ocean on a raft when even proper ships often get wrecked in storms. I'm not going unless you swear an oath that you are not planning more pain for me.'

She swore, and at dawn the next day took him to where suitable trees grew near the sea. She gave him a bronze axe, with which he cut down twenty trees. Also an adze for shaping the wood and a gimlet for boring holes to tie the trunks together. He covered the trunks with long planks, and set a mast at the centre with a yard arm and also a rudder. Calypso brought him cloth for the sails. The work took four days and when the raft was ready he launched it onto the sea, using levers. On the fifth day she dressed him in suitable clothing and they secured crates of food and bottles of water and wine onto the raft. Then she kissed him goodbye and sent him off with gentle, warm breezes.

Poseidon had not yet returned from Ethiopia so I took a risk and directed the raft towards the island of Scheria which was the home of the Phaeacians, a people whom I knew well. I thought that Odysseus might be able to reach Scheria in three or four days if all went well. Unfortunately Poseidon returned from Ethopia earlier than expected and happened to catch sight of the raft. He immediately knew what had happened and that the gods had seized the opportunity to help Odysseus while he was away. He sent a violent storm that churned up huge waves which struck the raft, smashing the mast and tiller and nearly drowning Odysseus who was weighed down by the clothes Calypso had given him, but managed to get back onto the damaged raft. After that, Poseidon went off to his palace in the sea thinking he'd done enough to give Aeneas more pain and trouble. But then the goddess Ino suddenly emerged from the sea. She had once been a mortal, the daughter of Cadmus who founded the city of Thebes. When her son was murdered by her own husband, Ino had tried to kill herself by jumping into the sea but the gods had taken pity on her and changed her into a sea-goddess. Now, having seen what Poseidon had done to Aeneas, and feeling sorry for him, she sat on the raft beside him and gave him some advice. She said he must abandon the wrecked raft and swim towards the nearest land whose mountain tops he could just see on the horizon. She lent him her scarf which she said would protect him from danger or death. When he reached the land he must throw it into the water and it would be returned to her. Then she dived back into the sea.

When I was sure Poseidon had gone home I came back

to see how I could further assist Odysseus. Having stripped off his clothes and tied Ino's scarf round him, he was starting to swim so I calmed the winds and smoothed the waves in front of him. I knew that the land Ino had pointed out was Phaeacia, and I made sure he swam in the right direction. The people there have always worshipped me. They have dedicated a temple and a grove to me, and Nausicaa, the young daughter of King Alcinous and Queen Arete, is my priestess. Furthermore, the Phaeacians were known for their kindness to any foreigners or beggars who might arrive on their shores. They were a sea-faring people and most likely they would send Odysseus on to Ithaca in one of their trading ships.

Towards the evening of the second day Odysseus was approaching the Phaeacian coastline although by now completely exhausted. But there was a problem. He could see a line of cliffs, but seemingly nowhere to land. Yet from above I noticed the estuary of a wide river so I persuaded the local river god to help. Between us we guided Odysseus towards the spot I had already chosen for him. He was able to swim a short way up the river and drag himself onto the bank, not forgetting to throw Ino's scarf back into the river from which it drifted out to sea where she could collect it. He found a densely forested patch of land next to the river and chose a spot well-hidden between the trees where there were piles of dead leaves with which to cover himself. I closed his eyes in sleep.

Then, the hardest part of my plan. I went to the palace when Nausicaa was asleep and crept past the guards at her bedroom door. I gave her a powerful dream in which her best friend came to see her and angered her by teasing her about the piles of dirty clothes that were lying about in her room.

In the dream I told her, 'Oh Nausicaa, don't be lazy. You'll soon be married so you need to keep your best clothes in pristine condition. First thing tomorrow ask your father if you can have the mule cart and servants to take all those dirty clothes to the washing pools beside the river.'

Dreams are tricky. For example, it took two attempts for the dream I gave Odysseus about the Trojan horse to properly get through and take root. The first time, when he woke, he only remembered something about a huge horse that could jump over the walls of Troy. I had to give him the dream all over again the following night. So when Nausicaa woke up I first thought she had entirely forgotten her dream, but then I heard her ask her father if she could borrow a cart and mules to transport dirty clothes to the pools.

The clothes to be washed were piled onto the cart which Nausicaa and her servant girls drove to the shallow freshwater pools beside the river mouth and close to where Odysseus had hidden himself. The girls released the mules and drove them to a grass meadow nearby to graze. They carried the clothes to the washing pools where they sang and danced as they trod on them until they were clean. Then they spread them out in the sun to dry while they went swimming and afterwards ate the lunch that Nausicaa's mother, Arete, had provided for them.

Odysseus was still asleep near the washing pool, and the servant girls, having packed the dried clothing onto the cart and harnessed the mules, were playing with a ball. It was thrown to one girl standing right beside the river who missed it and it fell into the water. They all screamed which woke Odysseus up. He emerged from the trees, naked and filthy with his hair encrusted with salt. All the girls ran away when they saw him except Nausicaa who waited to

135

see who he was. In this kind of situation he was always very plausible, so I left it up to him what he told her. He said he wondered if she might be a goddess, she was so beautiful. He was a penniless and ignorant stranger whose ship had been wrecked, and he had been washed up here by the sea. He appealed to her sympathy and she agreed to help and called on her servants to wash him and find some clothes for him. This is when I made the mistake of improving his appearance and making him look younger, when I knew perfectly well that Nausicaa was on the lookout for an interesting young husband. Perhaps I was trying to imitate Aphrodite and her love-making skills. Anyway, she was clearly attracted to this newly washed and youthful stranger. Later I heard her whisper to one of her servants that she'd love to marry someone like him.

Before climbing onto her cart Nausicaa explained to Odysseus how to get to her royal parents.

'The palace is in the middle of town,' she said. 'I won't offer you a lift because people will see us together and wonder who you are, and rumours will start flying around about how I've chosen you for a husband.'

She asked him to follow on foot behind the cart and the servants until she told him to stop.

'I'll drive on and you should wait a bit until we have gone. You can ask anybody if you get lost.'

Odysseus did as he was told. When they got near the town Nausicaa and her girls left him and drove on to the palace. Then I appeared, holding a water pitcher and looking like a young girl. He asked me to show him the way to the palace and I took him there, telling him on the way a little about the Phaeacians and their history. I advised him to go straight to Queen Arete who would probably be at her loom, and beg her to help him get back home.

'Whatever she suggests, the king will usually agree,' I told him.

I covered him in mist so no one else would see him entering the palace. When he met the royal couple they treated him very kindly, offering him food and wine and providing him with a comfortable bed for the night.

'We'll talk in the morning,' said Alcinous, 'then you can tell us who you are and how we can help you.'

The next day Odysseus was asked to recount the story of his wanderings to the king and queen and other Phaeacian leaders. As usual with him, it was a fairly egotistical account, not mentioning me or any other divine help, and the royal couple were clearly much impressed with their guest's abilities to survive his many hardships. They promised they would provide him with a ship to take him back to Ithaca the very next day if he so wanted. Then Alcinous made what must have seemed to the listeners a rather premature offer, considering he had only met this stranger the previous evening.

'Odysseus,' he said, 'I wish you would stay here and marry my own daughter. I would give you a home and wealth if you would like to stay. If not, we would obviously never keep you here against your will.'

Odysseus thanked the king but said he still wanted to return to his home. It was agreed that a ship would be prepared which would set off the following afternoon to take him to Ithaca. In the morning he was invited to attend the games which were due to take place on a field just outside the city walls.

I knew that what Odysseus told them about wanting to go home was true – throughout all the dangers and difficulties he had endured since leaving Troy he had always dreamed of returning to Ithaca and to Penelope. On the other hand, he was clearly attracted by Nausicaa's youth and beauty, and saw, too, that she was ready to fall in love with him. I realised my mistake in ever encouraging this relationship between Odysseus and Nausicaa. At any moment he might change his mind and agree to marry her, and then my long-time friend and supplicant, Penelope, would have found herself abandoned. And now there was yet another factor. Odysseus was aware by this time that there were several young men among the Phaeacian nobility who were suitors for Nausicaa. If he accepted the king's offer he would be hated by all of them. He would have gained a new set of enemies who perhaps would band together to kill him. Altogether, an awkward decision for him to make.

The next morning a large crowd watched the young athletes who competed in running, throwing the discus, wrestling, and other sports. Odysseus was invited to join in any of the events but at first he declined, saying he had suffered so much his only thought was to get back home. Then Euryalus, the winner of the wrestling contest, and whom everyone knew was the leading suitor for Nausicaa's hand, addressed him scornfully.

'Stranger, we all know your type. As captain of a merchant ship you roam the seas thinking only of your ill-gotten profits. You are certainly no athlete.'

Stirred to anger, Odysseus replied, 'Euryalus, your body looks strong but I think your mind is weak. Otherwise you would not choose to deliberately insult a visitor to this country about whom you know little. Now, despite my suffering, I will join in your games.'

So saying, he seized a discus and flung it further than all the other competitors had. Then he offered to take on anyone in any sport they chose. He excluded running since, he said, his legs had become weak after so long at sea. No one accepted the challenge, and after a demonstration of dancing by a team of boys and girls, the afternoon ended. The king asked Euryalus to apologise to their guest for his remarks, which he did, but Odysseus suspected that many of the other young men agreed with his attitude.

A ship with fifty-two rowers had been made ready to escort Odysseus to Ithaca. King Alcinous had asked all the Phaeacian nobles to give gifts to their guest on his departure, and he himself contributed many vessels and ornaments of silver and gold. Odysseus now was to meet Nausicaa for the last time. No doubt she still saw him as a potential husband but of course she could hardly say so unless he himself first showed any sign of wanting to stay in Scheria. As for Odysseus, by now he had made up his mind to leave the country as quickly as possible. I think that ever since Nausicaa had been offered to him in marriage by her father he had become wary of falling into another trap, just as first Circe and then Calypso had entrapped him. Therefore when it was time to say goodbye both of them were polite but cautious.

'Goodbye then, stranger,' she said. 'Remember me when you reach home, because you owe your life to me. I helped you first.'

'Nausicaa,' Odysseus replied, 'if Zeus ever permits me to go back and see my home, there I shall pray to you as to a god, since you saved my life.'

CHAPTER 15: HERA

AENEAS TO ITALY

From Carthage, the Trojans sailed northwards towards Italy, but a contrary wind soon forced them to change course. They decided to head for the Sicilian harbour belonging to the elderly Trojan, King Acestes, who had given them hospitality earlier in their travels, and on whose land the father of Aeneas had been buried. Acestes again welcomed his fellow countrymen, and with his consent Aeneas decided to celebrate sacred games in memory of his father. He led the men, young and old, to the tomb of Anchises beside which the games were to take place. The women, however, remained on the beach to look after the ships – and to remind each other how tired they all were of journeying across interminable seas without knowing what the end of it all would be.

From high above I noticed the beached ships and the crowd of women nearby, and I decided to act. I sent down my handmaiden, Iris, who took on the appearance of old Beröe, a much respected Trojan lady known to all. Iris rushed into the midst of the women and addressed them as follows: 'Women of Troy, this is the seventh summer since the fall of our city. Have we not had enough of being driven up and down by wind and storm across the angry seas? Now we find ourselves on land belonging to King Acestes, a fellow countryman who respects us and would help us to found a new city here. So what can we do to make Lord Aeneas give up his never-ending quest? Come with me and I will show you.'

She thrust a stick into a bonfire which the women had lit on the beach, set it ablaze, and then threw it with all her strength onto the nearest ship. Screaming and shouting, others joined her, and soon fire was licking along the whole line of Trojan ships. Unfortunately, just then Aeneas and the men returned from their games and saw the burning ships. They managed to put out the flames although four of the ships were beyond repair. Many of the women along with the older men now chose to stay on in Sicily rather than follow their selfish leader on any more of his adventures in foreign lands. And Acestes promised to help them build a new city on his land. Would that all the Trojans had made this choice. This would have spared the violence and bitterness that awaited them in Italy.

Many days later I happened to be crossing the skies above Latium when from far off I caught sight of the Trojan camp and the long black ships drawn up on the bank of the river Tiber. Then I noticed that messengers had been dispatched by Aeneas to visit King Latinus in his palace at the nearby city of Laurentium. He was the ruler of the territory where they had just landed. I followed these messengers whom Latinus received with much politeness and even enthusiasm when he heard who they were and where they had come from. The king also gave the messengers some surprising news. He claimed that when recently visiting the tomb of his father in the nearby woods he had heard his father's voice warning him that no one from Latium must be permitted to marry his young daughter and heiress, Lavinia. Instead, she must marry a stranger who had only recently arrived in the country. Then Latinus told the messengers he hoped to meet their leader as soon as possible. Straight away I realised what the old king was considering – a marriage between Lavinia and Aeneas – so I became determined to prevent this at all costs. I knew Lavinia had already been promised to Turnus, the young king of the Rutulians from just south of Latium. Turnus was Queen Amata's nephew, a handsome young man and reputedly an excellent warrior. Turnus had visited King Latinus and asked for his daughter's hand in marriage. Amata was particularly keen on this marriage, and said so frequently. In fact she was so keen that it sometimes seemed to visitors that she was herself in love with her nephew. But Lavinia did not want to marry anyone, particularly not Turnus whom she thought brash, self-confident and insensitive.

I thought it was ridiculous that a complete stranger from the other side of the world could suddenly appear in Latium, disrupt previous arrangements, and immediately receive special favour from this elderly king just because the king claimed to have received a vision. I decided to lend my support to Turnus in the conflict I could see approaching.

From the underworld I called out Alecto, one of the Furies, who owed me a few favours. Her speciality was war, havoc and destruction, and I told her exactly what I wanted. First, Alecto poisoned the mind of Latinus's wife, Queen Amata, so that she was ready to disobey her husband's plans for her daughter's marriage to Aeneas.

Alecto incited Amata to argue bitterly with Latinus. She told him that his so-called vision – that only a foreigner might marry his daughter – must have been merely a dream, or rather a nightmare. Then she reminded him they had already promised Turnus he could marry Lavinia, and they could hardly go back on their word. Also, that Ardea, the city which Turnus and his Rutulians came from, wasn't actually part of Latium, so Turnus might still be the foreigner the vision meant. Finally, that Turnus was the perfect husband for Lavinia, but he was also a very proud young man, and would most likely declare war on them if they allowed someone else to marry her. None of these arguments, however, carried the slightest weight with the old king so Amata decided on something more drastic. She had Lavinia seized and hidden in the nearby woods, and she sent a messenger to Turnus that he should come and marry her straight away – by force, if necessary.

Next, Alecto brought about an incident which even the most peaceful Latin might regard as a legitimate cause for war. She persuaded a Trojan hunting party led by young Ascanius, the son of Aeneas, to kill a huge white stag that was sleeping in the forest. This animal had been brought up by the daughter of King Latinus's chief herdsman after its mother died, and it had long been regarded as a special – even a sacred – beast by the farmers of Latium. And finally, I infected Turnus with a bitter hatred of the new arrivals, and inspired him to summon all available forces for an attack on the Trojan camp beside the Tiber. Now a war frenzy gripped the Latins and the Rutulians, and all the able-bodied men collected at Laurentium, preparing to cross the plain and besiege the Trojans. Old King Latinus was dismayed by the turn of events, but felt too tired and weak to oppose the popular mood, and did nothing except shut himself away in his palace. And when I heard that Aeneas had left his camp and travelled up river in a search for allies, I advised Turnus to attack without delay.

During the whole course of the war between Italians and Trojans that followed, I and my rival Aphrodite were closely involved, both of us observing the fighting from above, one on each side. However, we were both also aware of how angry Zeus had been with gods and goddesses who had participated in the Trojan war so we did not dare to use weapons, but we each looked after our respective heroes, Turnus and Aeneas, and tried to shield them from danger. I, for instance, once protected Turnus from drowning after he had flung himself into the sea in full armour to escape his enemies. At another time I deflected a Trojan arrow which was flying straight for him. And when Aeneas was wounded in the arm by an arrow shot from an unknown bow, it was Aphrodite who cured his wound with that magic herb, dittany. After hours of bitter conflict in which many from both sides lost their lives, Turnus and his Rutulians successfully breached the gates of the enemy camp and forced an entry. It seemed as though all was over for the Trojans. But things were about to change for them with the arrival of reinforcements.

As I was starting to watch the battle inside the camp, suddenly a great shout of triumph rose from those guarding the Trojan walls. They had seen the flash of bronze from a shield held aloft from a ship approaching down the river. It was from the shield of Aeneas, and behind him sailed a long line of ships belonging to his new allies, the Etruscans. Next to Aeneas stood a young man dressed in new, sparkling armour. This was Pallas, the young son of King Evander, who ruled a small kingdom on the other side of the Tiber from Etruria. Pallas had been entrusted to the care of Aeneas by his father, and he was looking forward to experiencing his first battle. Once the new arrivals had beached their ships beside the Trojan camp the course of the battle swung the other way. By nightfall the Trojans had ejected their enemies from the camp and pushed them back across the ditches. The fighting ended as night fell, to be resumed early the next morning.

Another day of ceaseless conflict saw the front line between the two sides shift back and forth across the plain. The Etruscans proved to be experienced warriors. It was our bad luck that they had ever agreed to join in a war which I had thought did not concern them. The reason they were there was their hatred of their former king. For many years, King Mezentius had been a ruthless dictator. He had tortured anyone who got in his way, and had shown himself a monster of cruelty. He had even devised a horrific new way of killing. He would bind the victim to a decaying corpse, hand to hand and face to face, and let the poison of the embrace bring about a lingering death. Finally, due to the universal hatred he had inspired, Mezentius had fled from Etruria, and Turnus had offered him asylum. Now he was helping Turnus in the war, and this was enough for the Etruscans to support the Trojans.

Turnus, the Rutulian leader, was so infected by the spirit of war that he appeared to lose all caution. He shouted challenges at his enemies, thus calling attention to himself and constantly attracting their numerous spears and arrows. Many Trojans and Etruscans fell to his own spear or sword, and he showed no mercy to those he had wounded, even when they surrendered to him and begged for their lives. This was what happened to Pallas, the young son of King Evander. In spite of his plea for mercy Turnus slew him with one thrust of his sword and then made what later proved to be a major blunder by tearing off the handsome baldric worn by his victim and tying it onto his own shoulder.

When the battle seemed to be turning against the Italians I devised a complicated plan to get Turnus out of danger. I fashioned an effigy of Aeneas out of empty vapour, copying his features, his armour, and even the crest on his helmet, and I gave this weird phantom the power to speak, though not to reason – like the figures we meet in our dreams. I placed it in the Trojan front line where it pranced around brandishing its weapons and shouting obscenities and challenges across at Turnus who was goaded into throwing his spear at it from long range. The apparition turned tail and fled leading Turnus to believe Aeneas was frightened and running away from him. He drew his sword and ran in pursuit, taunting his quarry as he ran.

'Where are you running to, Aeneas?' he shouted. 'My sword will soon give your dead body a portion of the land you have come so far to rule.'

I chose one of the moored Etruscan ships that had a ladder tied from its deck to the beach, and I made the panic-stricken phantom climb along this ladder and hide itself in the ship, closely followed by Turnus. Then I cut the ship's moorings and took it out towards the open sea on the receding tide. Meanwhile Turnus ran round the ship looking for the phantom which had disappeared into the air, while the ship drifted further out to sea. Soon he realised he had somehow been tricked, and that both sides in the conflict would think him a coward for running away. With a little help from me he managed to jump off the ship, armour and all, and swim back to the nearest beach, but by that time it was getting dark and the fighting was over for the day.

The next morning the Trojan and Etruscan forces advanced across the plain as far as the walls of Laurentium and they succeeded in breaking open the main gate and entering the city. Chaotic scenes followed, but Aeneas was able to take command and make himself heard by both sides. He announced that the war was now over. Its result would be decided by a combat between himself and Turnus. Personally, I was not happy with this suggestion, not because I doubted Turnus's skill or his courage but rather because I had heard about the armour and weapons which Hephaestus had forged for Aeneas. I knew that this divine armour could not be pierced by any arrow or bronze spear. However, there was little I could say or do.

It was now that Zeus saw me watching the scene below from a golden cloud and he summoned me to his side. He said, 'My dear wife, what do you expect to achieve by perching there high up in those chilly clouds? The time has come for you to end your support for Turnus. You have harried Aeneas and his Trojans over land and sea, and have succeeded in kindling an unholy war in Latium. The end has now come. I forbid you to go further.'

'Dread lord and husband,' I replied, 'obviously I have to obey your command. But I entreat you to allow what the Fates do not forbid. When peace has been established between the two sides, do not force the people of Latium to change their customs and their language, their ancient name and native dress. After all, Troy has fallen. So make it the Trojans who change, not the Latins.'

Zeus smiled and said, 'Let it be so. I will make these two peoples speak the same language and share the same customs. And you will see that no other race of mortals will be their equal in paying honour to the gods.'

So in this way I was forced to abandon my support for

the Latin and Rutulian people, and allow a group of strangers to share their land.

I watched the duel between the two heroes with sadness since I felt sure how it would end. Turnus, without me to protect him, was easy prey. After he broke his own sword in trying to find a way through Aeneas's godlike armour he was handed another, but instead of using it he picked up a huge stone and tried to throw it at his opponent. The task was too much for him, and the stone fell to earth before reaching its target. Then Aeneas threw his mighty spear which penetrated Turnus's armour and fixed itself in his thigh. He fell to his knees and Aeneas stood over him with sword raised to strike. Turnus begged for mercy and Aeneas hesitated but then caught sight of the baldric of Pallas that Turnus was wearing. Burning with mad passion he plunged his sword into Turnus's breast. I could not bear to see any more. I left my cloud and returned to my palace in Olympia.

CHAPTER 16: APHRODITE

AENEAS WINS

I accompanied the Trojan fleet from Carthage remaining hidden throughout the journey, although probably Aeneas knew I was there. When the wind suddenly changed, forcing the fleet to land on a beach in Sicily, I wondered whether Poseidon might be up to his old tricks. But when I mingled with the women arguing on the beach, and saw them setting fire to the ships, I realised that Hera was behind it. Luckily, soon after the women had started the fires, the men returned, having finished their games. With my help they were able to staunch the flames, although it then took several days to repair the ships, and four of them turned out to be beyond saving. The women who, driven mad by Iris and Hera, had tried to destroy their own vessels were now forgiven, and all the Trojans, men and women, were offered a choice: those wishing to stay in Sicily would be allowed to do so. Acestes, the Trojan king who ruled the land where the ships were beached, promised he would help them to build and fortify a new settlement, a second Troy. But those who chose to follow Aeneas would now voyage onwards to new lands, and this was easily the majority.

While the repairs were going on I returned to Olympia. I felt there was not much point in talking to Hera, so instead I went to see Poseidon.

'Hera will never give up her hatred of the Trojans until she has wrecked their ships and drowned them all,' I told him. 'But surely you, not she, is supposed to be in charge of the oceans. I beg you to allow these sorrowful survivors from Troy, who have suffered so much, to sail to the River Tiber and so complete what the Fates have ordained. Grant them following winds and a safe journey.'

And Lord Poseidon agreed to my request. I knew he was not one to ignore what the Fates had decreed – unlike the Queen of the gods.

I followed the Trojan fleet all the way from Sicily, up the west coast of Italy until we reached the mouth of the river Tiber. We entered the estuary and sailed up the river. The kingdom of Etruria was now on our north bank and Latium to the south. A few miles upstream I gave Aeneas a sign that we should anchor and set up our camp beside the water. I told him to send messengers to inform King Latinus who we were, and to request permission for us to remain on his land which he gave.

I learned that Latinus had been a warrior when he was younger, he had fought wars to establish his kingdom, but now he was elderly and tired. His wife, Amata, was a Rutulian princess from Ardea, not far to the south. She had borne him two sons and a daughter, but the boys had both died very young, leaving only Lavinia. Their deaths had so affected Amata that she never recovered from her depression and anger. She treated her young daughter harshly, seeming to blame her for surviving when her brothers had not. But King Latinus did his best to humour his wife, avoiding confrontation whenever possible.

It was this royal family – Latinus, his wife Amata, their daughter Lavinia and her suitor Turnus – who were to be used by Hera as pawns in the war that soon followed our arrival in Latium.

Latinus welcomed with courtesy the messengers sent by Aeneas and agreed to their request that the Trojan arrivals might be allowed a strip of land beside the Tiber on which to set up a walled camp. The relationship between Trojans and Latins seemed to be one of friendship and peace, but sadly this was not to last.

I had not been able to prevent Hera from goading the Italians into war. All I could do was to beg my husband Hephaestus, who was blacksmith to the gods, to forge Aeneas a new set of armour which no bronze sword could penetrate, and a great shield which few men apart from him could easily lift. On the shield were engraved numerous small scenes predicting future events that were not easy to interpret. Early one morning the Trojans saw in the distance the clouds of dust which indicated the approach of an enemy army across the plain. They had time to close the gates and man the ramparts of their walled camp before it was surrounded. Unfortunately, it was at this moment that Aeneas himself was away from the camp. He had learnt that war was approaching and had sailed up-river in a search for possible allies, He went to Evander, king of a small city on one side of the Tiber, and then on to the large kingdom of Etruria on the other side. He left his young son, Ascanius, in charge, hoping all would be quiet until he got back.

A long and brutal contest started. The Trojans were very much in the minority; on the other hand their force contained many experienced veterans who had defended their city from the Greeks all during the ten-year Trojan war. But gradually the enemy pushed forward, across the ditch and right up to the main gate, in spite of the showers of spears and arrows directed at them from the ramparts. A small group of Rutulians eventually forced open the main gate and entered the camp. They were led by Turnus who held a flaming torch in his hand. His plan was to prevent any chance of the Trojans escaping by sea by setting fire to their line of ships beached nearby. Yet in his wild ambition he overreached himself. Harassed by Trojan spears and swords he tried to hide himself in one of the Trojan ships. Hera was on hand to help his flight, though I'm not quite sure how she did it. I think she must have cut the ropes that anchored the ship where he was hiding so that it was blown out to sea, and later saved him from drowning when he tried to swim to a nearby beach in full armour – by which time fighting had ended for the day.

Just when a Trojan defeat was beginning to seem inevitable, Zeus summoned a council of all the gods to his palace in Olympus. When they were seated he addressed them all.

'Oh great dwellers in the sky, why do you contend with such bitterness? I thought I had forbidden Italians to clash with the Trojans. Why is there such discord against my express wishes?'

I rose to my feet. 'Dear Father of all gods and mortals,' I said, 'Turnus and his Rutulians are rampant. They have entered the gates of the new Trojan camp, and the ditches, so recently dug, are filling up with Trojan blood. Aeneas is far away and has left his young son in charge, facing overwhelming odds. So it seems you have now changed your mind concerning my dear son and his destiny in Italy. Can this be true, and is it now your intention that this pitiful remnant of the Trojan people quit Italy for good? Or are they to be wiped out and their ships burnt?'

Hera was wild with rage. 'Aphrodite,' she exclaimed, 'you are the goddess of love, not war. You know nothing about nations, their quarrels and their rights. All you want is to protect your own selfish son. He is the aggressive one, not Turnus. If your son decides to cross the world and seize the land of a people he had never previously heard of – then it may not be possible to protect him. Turnus and his people have lived in this country for generations. Are they supposed to welcome these foreigners and yield to their unlawful demands? No, they will resist them as best they can.

'Why,' she asked, turning towards the assembled gods, 'did Aeneas ever decided to sail to Italy in the first place? Could he not have stayed with Acestes in Sicily, as did many Trojan women? Better still, could he and his followers not have remained hidden on Mount Ida until the Greeks had gone, and then rebuilt Troy?'

I tried to explain how it was Aeneas's divine destiny to found a new kingdom beside the Tiber, and that this kingdom would one day become an empire that ruled the world.

To this Hera gave a sneering laugh. 'Divine destiny indeed!' she snorted. 'It was Cassandra and her ravings that prompted him to sail to Italy and seize land that belonged to other people.'

I pointed out that Cassandra had nothing to do with it since Apollo had ensured that no one would ever believe her prophesies. Then I turned to Zeus.

'Almighty king,' I said, 'I beg you to ask your cruel wife how long she will go on persecuting these pitiful survivors of the war against Troy. Is it not enough for her that Troy has been burnt and its people enslaved?'

Again Hera interrupted me. 'If we are to go back to the

Trojan war,' she said, looking round at her divine audience for support, 'ought we not to remember how that war started? Was it I who helped that Trojan adulterer, Paris, steal the wife of King Menelaus and carry her off to Troy? No, it was you, Aphrodite, because you promised Paris that he could have Helen.'

In the end Zeus put a stop to these arguments and delivered his judgement. He said he could see we would never agree with each other, so his decision was that we just let the two sides continue their war without our interference. This was a disastrous conclusion because, in spite of what had happened to Turnus, the Rutulians were clearly about to capture the Trojan camp, and no god was to be allowed to stop them. Hera had won the discussion. However, when I returned to my post of observation above the battlefield I was much reassured. A long line of black warships was approaching the Trojan camp with Aeneas visible at the helm of the leading ship. He was back, and he had clearly succeeded in gaining some powerful allies. The ships were beached close to the Trojan camp, and the tide of battle now turned decisively in the Trojans' favour.

The following morning I observed the movement of the front line as it shifted away from the Trojan ramparts and across the plain separating Laurentium and the sea. I was disturbed by having to witness the ferocity of the battle. As usual it was the sad sight of men slaughtering each other amid the blaring of trumpets and the shouts and screams of the warriors. I found this particular battle more disturbing than most because my son, infected by the madness of war, was rushing from place to place, inflicting death by spear or sword on any who crossed his path. His followers were close behind him, trying to strip the blood-stained armour from those who fell, even before they were dead. Among the many whom Aeneas killed was Mezentius, the former merciless dictator of Etruria, along with his young son, Lausus, who fell trying to protect his father. Although I admit I was pleased that the Trojans and their allies the Etruscans now seemed to be forcing their enemies back, away from the camp, I was disturbed to witness Aeneas's passionate bloodlust.

'Is my son, then, what mortals call a war hero?' I asked myself.

Elsewhere on the battlefield Turnus was doing just the same to Trojans and Etruscans, though the paths of the two leaders never seemed to cross. I saw Turnus rush at Pallas, the young prince whom King Evander, his father, had entrusted to Aeneas's care. Pallas fought bravely but soon fell to Turnus's sword. Then Turnus tore the decorated baldric from off the shoulder of the dying Pallas, and put it on himself.

After many hours of fighting the tide of war eventually turned conclusively against the Rutulians and Latins, many of whom gave up the conflict and rushed for safety into Laurentium. I put it into the head of Aeneas that now, while its defences were in turmoil, was the moment to attack the city. The Trojans forced their way to the main gate, overwhelmed the guard and entered the city. Chaos and confusion ensued, but those watching from the ramparts now grasped that the war was lost. At this moment a new misfortune overtook the citizens. Their queen, Amata, when she saw Aeneas victorious, knew that all her hopes for the future were in ruins, and in her rage and depression she took her own life. Her women found her body hanging from the noose she had made of twisted cloth, and tied over a beam. Her death was entirely due to that wicked plot between Alecto and Hera.

Zeus who had been watching the course of the battle and the entry of the Trojans and their allies into the Latium capital, now called his wife to him. He told her she must finally abandon her intervention in the war, and her support for Turnus – and she promised to obey. Meanwhile, in Laurentium it had been agreed that the outcome of the war would be decided by a personal combat between the two champions, Aeneas and Turnus. A space was cleared outside the city gates, and the soldiers from both armies formed a ring as spectators. The combat did not last very long, ending when Aeneas threw his mighty spear at his opponent. It pierced the outer ring of his shield and went through the middle of his thigh. Down went great Turnus, bending his knee to the ground. He lowered his eyes and stretched out his hand to beg for mercy.

'You have defeated me,' he said, 'so for myself I ask nothing. But if any thought of my unhappy father can move you, then spare my life for his sake. You had such a father in Anchises. And if it is your will to kill me, then at least give him back my body.'

Aeneas was standing above Turnus with his sword raised ready to strike, but these words caused him to pause. He slowly lowered the sword, and it seemed that Turnus would be spared. But then Aeneas saw the baldric which had belonged to young Pallas, and which Turnus now boastfully wore on his own shoulder as a battle honour. Trembling with mad passion, Aeneas thrust his sword into his powerless victim's chest, shouting, 'I give you this in memory of Pallas whom you robbed and killed.'

On the death of Turnus the war came to a speedy end with the Latins and Rutulians recognising the right of the Trojans to build a city close to their existing camp on the river. The new city was to be named Lavinium after King

Lavinus's daughter, and construction was soon underway. And, as the king had promised, Lavinia married Aeneas and they were recognised by all as successors to the kingdom of Latium when the old king died.

Soon after the marriage I decided to pay a visit to see whether the bloodlust I had observed in Aeneas when he murdered his enemy had now dissipated, and whether he had succeeded in adapting himself to a peaceful domestic existence. I flew down to Lavinium, and walked invisibly past streets full of empty plots, half-built homes, and workmen on scaffolding. The largest plot was clearly planned to be the site of a temple, and the only completed building was the royal palace, set on a rise overlooking the rest of the town. I entered the front door, noting Aeneas's armour and the enormous shield made by Hephaestus hanging in the hallway. Lavinia was alone at her loom so I revealed myself to her and asked her how life married to a hero suited her. She fell to her knees in front of me with tears in her eyes.

'I love him.' she said, 'and I have never been so happy in my whole life. Your son is so kind and sensitive. He may be twice my age but we are partners in everything.'

I was much reassured by her words and we went on to have a long conversation, partly about how men seemed to be able to lose themselves in the madness of war one day, and turn into peaceful family men the next. Lavinia told me about the tasks they had set themselves: supervising the construction of the new city, helping Trojans and Latins to work and live together, and maintaining a close relationship with King Latinus in Laurentium. She thanked me for always protecting Aeneas in times of war and peace, and explained that the temple they were building in Lavinium would be dedicated to me. Of course what I did not tell her was something I had learnt from Hera: that their married life would be brief. Aeneas, having succeeded old Latinus as king the following year, would himself sadly die three years later. It turned out Lavinia was already pregnant when I made my visit, so before I left the palace we went to look at the scenes of the future depicted on the shield, and I explained how her son would be the ancestor of a famous line of kings who would one day rule a vast city called Rome whose influence would spread across the world.

CHAPTER 17: ATHENA

ODYSSEUS RETURNS HOME

At the time Odysseus was being held captive by Calypso I had arranged with Zeus that I would go to Ithaca to meet Telemachus, Odysseus's young son. I promised I would bolster his courage so that he might dare to challenge the crowd of suitors who were harassing his mother, Penelope. They were demanding she pick one of them to marry, since her husband was certainly dead by now. Zeus, for his part, promised to send his messenger, Hermes, to tell Calypso it was high time she let Odysseus go. I flew down to Ithaca and entered the palace, disguised as Mentor, an old friend of Odysseus and his father. There I found the suitors sitting around waiting for their evening banquet to be served. They were shouting and laughing at each other's jokes. Telemachus was sitting with them, silent and dejected. He was a handsome young man who looked very much like Odysseus, although considerably taller. When he saw me he immediately called me over in keeping with the laws of hospitality.

'Good evening, stranger, and welcome,' he said. 'Be our guest, come share our meal and then tell us how we can help you.'

I took the seat he indicated and was served with rich food and wine.

Telemachus then sat down beside me and we spoke, quietly, so that no one else could hear us.

'I am Mentor,' I explained. 'Your father and I have been close friends since before you were born. I came to the palace today hoping to meet him, but I hear his homecoming has yet again been delayed. But who are all these young men who seem to be enjoying your hospitality? They certainly make enough noise.'

At this, Telemachus released all his anger and resentment against the suitors: 'They are selfish young noblemen from Ithaca and nearby islands who turn up every day to feast at our expense. They say that my mother must choose one of them as a husband, and until she does they will not go away. They are wasting away our whole estate and my mother can do nothing. If only my father were here he would know how to deal with them, but I'm certain that by now he has either drowned or been killed in battle. I myself am too young and weak to resist them, and I am all on my own.'

He asked me for my advice and I told him I felt certain his father was alive and would be coming home shortly. Until then he must be brave. I suggested he find a suitable ship and crew and sailed to Pylos on the mainland to consult Nestor, a wise old leader and a close companion of Odysseus during the Trojan war. If anyone knew where his father was now it would be Nestor.

It was possible that Telemachus suspected I was not

Mentor at all, but a god in disguise; in any case he followed my advice. When the suitors had finished their banquet he told them he was leaving Ithaca to sail to Pylos and then to Sparta seeking news of his father. When he came back he would decide what to do next. They laughed at him, not believing he was capable of carrying out such a plan.

'Oh no!' they sneered. 'Telemachus is planning to kill us. Perhaps he will bring back lethal poison from Pylos to mix in our wine bowls.'

At this point I left the palace, determined to play my part in this new adventure. Still disguised as Mentor, I persuaded a rich merchant who knew me to lend us a ship, and I went through the town calling for volunteers to man her. Then I returned to the palace and poured sleep into the eyes of those suitors who had not yet left for their homes. Telemachus asked his old nurse Eurycleia, who was in charge of the storerooms, to help him pack food in leather bags and wine in barrels for his trip. At first she did her best to persuade him not to go.

'Sweet child, whatever gave you this idea? Do not go searching for danger out on the restless sea. Stay with us who love you.'

But when he told her that he suspected a goddess was on his side she agreed to help. He begged her not to tell his mother where he was going and she promised not to. Meanwhile, in the dead of night I assembled our crew and had them drag the beached ship into the water and rig it. Some of them I sent to collect from the palace the stores that Eurycleia had collected, and when all was ready I sat down in the stern next to Telemachus and we started our journey.

During all the time I spent with Telemachus, his father was on his way back to his wife and home. The Phaeacian sailors took Odysseus to Ithaca, though he was so exhausted from his recent sporting achievements that he slept on the deck during the entire journey. When he woke up he found himself alone on dry land, with all the gifts the Phaeacian nobles had given him piled up beside him. At first he had no idea where he was and felt sure the sailors had left him on the wrong island, but then I appeared disguised as a young shepherd, and he begged for my help, telling me a long made-up story of who he was and how he had got here from Crete. I removed my disguise and addressed him.

'You cunning liar! Do you not recognise me now? I am Athena, daughter of Zeus. I have always taken care of you, in all your hardships.'

But he was still wary. 'I do know you helped me during the war against Troy,' he said, 'but where were you after the war, when all our ships were battered by terrible storms sent by the gods?'

I explained that my absence then was because I did not want to conflict with Poseidon who resented him because he had blinded his son, Polyphemus. Then we discussed the situation in the palace; how young noblemen from Ithaca and the neighbouring islands had collected together, each hoping to marry Penelope, since everyone thought Odysseus was dead. Every night these suitors feasted on animals from his flocks and herds. They seduced the female servants, and generally made a nuisance of themselves while Penelope kept to her room because there was little she could do to stop them.

I explained how I had accompanied Telemachus to visit old Nestor in Pylos, and then how Telemachus had continued his journey to meet Menelaus in Sparta. His purpose had been to try and find out whether or not his father was still alive. Odysseus was surprised when I told him, 'You knew perfectly well I was alive. Why did you send Telemachus off on such a long and dangerous journey for nothing?'

'Don't worry about the boy,' I told him. 'He enjoyed meeting Nestor and Menelaus. And a voyage like that helps him mature and become more confident. Anyway, now you are here I shall go to Sparta and tell him to return home as quickly as possible. Then the two of you can decide what to do about the suitors.'

We discussed our future plans and I warned him not to tell anyone yet that he had arrived in Ithaca, not even his wife. I turned him into an old beggar with wrinkled skin and a bent back. His clothes I changed into a tattered cloak and ragged tunic. I advised him to search out Eumaeus, his father's swineherd, who was well known for his hospitality towards strangers and beggars. Perhaps he would be allowed to stay in the swineherd's hut and he could wait there for Telemachus to appear.

Then I flew off to Sparta to meet Telemachus whom I found enjoying his stay in the palace of Menelaus and his queen, Helen, both of whom had returned from Troy after the war. I told Telemachus he must hurry back to Ithaca where soon he would meet his father. But I also warned him that the suitors were planning to kill him on his way home. They had a ship which was anchored off the island of Same waiting to ambush him as he sailed from Pylos. He must therefore find a new route back which avoided that island. And when he reached Ithaca he must not return straight away to the palace but first must go to see Eumaeus who had known him since he was a baby, and would certainly receive him with hospitality.

All went well. Eumaeus was overjoyed to meet

Telemachus and offered him a meal and a bed for the night. They had a long conversation in which the swineherd said what a kind master Odysseus had been, but that by now he was sure he was dead. At dawn he went off to choose a pig for the suitors' evening feast, as he had been ordered, and Telemachus was left alone in the hut. There came a knock at the door; it was a wrinkled old man begging for food. He was invited in but suddenly there was a flash of light and the ancient beggar changed into an elegantly dressed, younger man who held out his arms to Telemachus with a welcoming smile. This was my work, though neither of them could see me do it. Telemachus stepped back in confusion.

'Stranger, you look so different from before. Your clothes, your skin – I think you must be some god. Be kind to me and pity me.'

'I am no god,' Odysseus replied, 'I am your father, and after nearly twenty years I have come home. As for the way I look – Athena did it. She can transform me as she likes, sometimes a homeless beggar, sometimes a nobleman. For heavenly gods it is not difficult.'

Telemachus was convinced, and they kissed each other, tears pouring down their cheeks.

Afterwards they discussed what to do about the suitors. Odysseus said not to tell anyone he was back home until the right moment came – not even the swineherd, and not Penelope. That evening I visited the hut again to transform Odysseus back into a beggar, and Eumaeus also returned when he had delivered his pig. At dawn the next day Telemachus left for the palace to tell his mother he was back from his trip, and later Eumaeus and the old beggar (Odysseus) followed them. Penelope was reassured to see her son alive since she had heard about the intended ambush, and after greeting his mother he joined the suitors in the dining hall. Then the old beggar arrived at the palace and started going round the suitors asking for food. Telemachus had to pretend he didn't know who he was. All of them gave him something to put in his satchel – except Antinous, the most aggressive of the suitors, who instead threw a stool at his head. Sitting upstairs in her room, as she usually did when the suitors were stuffing themselves with her food, Penelope was told about the beggar and wanted to question him as to whether he had heard anything about her husband. But she had to wait until the feast was over and the guests had left.

I see that so far I have said a lot about Odysseus, but nothing about his unhappy wife. Since Odysseus went off to war, Penelope had successfully run the estate and the palace on her own, living in her home without a husband, watching Telemachus grow from a baby into a child, and then a handsome youth, wondering whether they would ever see his father again. The bards all sing of the bravery of heroes and the greatness of Odysseus's deeds, but no one sings of the courage required by those who were left behind. That also takes a hero's disposition.

Over the years I have received many prayers from Penelope. After Odysseus left she used to pray for his safety and his quick return to Ithaca, but more recently her prayers concerned her son who, as he grew up, had become more assertive and difficult for her to deal with. He was starting to challenge the suitors openly and she worried that one day they would have had enough, and decide to kill him (which of course they did try to do). Her prayers to me have also been about how she herself should deal with the suitors, and more particularly how to postpone the day when she was forced to agree to marry one of them. So, many moons ago I gave her a dream in which I suggested a solution to this particular problem. She must start weaving what she told everyone was to be a winding sheet for Laertes, her elderly father-in-law, whose death could not be far off. Then every night she should unpick what had been woven that day, so that the shroud was never completed. Not until this pious work was finished, she should tell them, could she possibly think of marrying anyone. For a long time this scheme worked very well – until someone told the suitors what she was up to.

Altogether there were about fifty servants working in the palace, and of these Penelope had twelve favourites. They were young slave girls who had been with her all their lives, and she trusted them. They were in on the secret of the shroud, and every night they came to her room to help unpick the day's work, and to give her any news or gossip.

'You are my spies,' she would say, 'and I'm relying on you to tell me what those suitors are up to. Get to know them well, and if necessary pretend you are in love with them. If they think you are on their side they'll tell you their plans.'

By the way, this wasn't as shocking as it might seem. I gather it was not unusual in a great household for the guests to sleep with the maids. This was seen as a part of good hospitality – so long as it was with the permission of the master of the house. Here, of course, there was no master around to give permission.

To return to the old beggar. When the feast was over and the suitors had departed to their own homes, Penelope came downstairs to question him about Odysseus. He spun her a story about how he came from Crete, and how once, before the Trojan war, Odysseus had stayed at his father's mansion. But Penelope was already beginning to suspect that the beggar might her husband in disguise. To check her theory, and knowing that Odysseus had a long scar on his leg where he had once been gashed by a wild boar, she asked old Eurycleia to wash the beggar's feet. Eurycleia brought a basin of hot water and started washing. She saw the scar, and knocked over the basin in her astonishment. Odysseus made her promise not to tell anyone, but Penelope had already noticed, though she decided to keep her knowledge secret until her husband revealed himself. Night was now approaching so everyone retired to their beds, the suitors to their homes, and I to Olympus. The old beggar was given a pile of sheep skins to lie on outside in the porch.

The next morning the suitors came back to the palace expecting their lunch, and I returned, much looking forward to the ensuing battle. I told Odysseus to reveal his true identity to his loyal followers, Eumaeus and his friend, a neighbouring cowherd. As proof he was to show them the scar on his leg, and ask for their help. I put into Penelope's mind a convincing scheme. She took from the storeroom Odysseus's great bow which only he had ever used, with a quiver full of arrows. She also collected twelve bronze axe heads, each with a ring at its back, but without their wooden handles. These were positioned in a row so that the rings were neatly lined up. Then she announced to the suitors,

'I feel sure that Odysseus is dead, and now is the time for me to decide on my new husband. This is his bow. If anyone can string it as he could, and can shoot an arrow through all twelve of these rings, I promise to marry him.'

By now the spears which usually decorated the walls of the dining hall had been quietly removed, as were any weapons which the suitors had brought with them and left at the back of the room. The door into the courtyard had

167

been bolted from the outside. There was now only one exit from the hall, and in front of its raised threshold stood Odysseus, Telemachus and their two servants. I was with them, again disguised as Mentor. Penelope now retired to her room, and the door to the women's quarters was securely locked.

Several of the suitors and also Telemachus attempted in turn to string the bow, but they all failed. Then Odysseus cried, 'Pass me the bow and I will see if any of my youthful strength still remains.'

The suitors clamoured that a foreign beggar had no right to touch such a sacred object, but Telemachus said it was up to him who might handle the bow, and ordered the swineherd to pass it over. Odysseus examined the bow carefully, and then bent and strung it with ease. He shot an arrow that passed through the twelve rings. A second arrow he aimed at Antinous, the suitor who had insulted him the most. He was sitting at his table sipping a goblet of red wine, with no thought of death. The arrow struck him in the throat and he slumped over the table spilling his wine which mixed with the blood gushing from his nose and mouth. The suitors could not believe what they were seeing, and first they thought it must be a gruesome accident. They shouted, 'Stranger, you have killed the best young man in Ithaca.'

Odysseus scowled at them. 'Dogs! So you thought I would never come back from Troy. You too must die. You have fleeced my house, flirted with my wife and raped my slave girls. Now you are trapped.'

Fear seized them all. They looked round for spears but there were none. Those who still had their swords now drew them and advanced towards the group guarding the door, trying to use their tables as shields. But Odysseus continued relentlessly to shoot his arrows, each one finding its mark. Telemachus and the others speared any suitor who got too close to the threshold, and I deflected any sword thrusts they might have missed. In less than an hour every suitor was either dead or badly injured and the floor was covered in blood. Odysseus in his rage wandered round the hall spearing bodies that showed any sign of life, while Penelope remained in her room and I returned to Olympia.

Odysseus now summoned old Eurycleia who was in charge of all the palace servants, and asked her to send to him any of them who had slept with one of the suitors. She sent down the twelve young girls with whom Penelope had spent many nights unwinding her tapestry, and whom she had trusted to be her spies. They were ordered to remove the bodies lying in the hall, and to mop up the blood from the floor. When they had finished, Odysseus ordered his son to take them outside with their hands tied behind their backs, and kill them all because they had been guilty of dishonouring him as master of the house. Telemachus strung a rope across the courtyard, then tied a noose around the neck of each servant, and attached each noose to the rope. He then pulled the rope with all his strength and re-tied the end of it to a wall. The girls' feet left the ground and the nooses were tightened by the weight of their bodies dangling in the air. All were gradually strangled to death.

I was disgusted when I became aware of these unjust and brutal murders. I heard Odysseus trying to justify his behaviour by arguing that these slave girls had besmirched his honour by giving their bodies to the suitors. But what is honour? It's not something we immortals have any knowledge of. Whatever it is I'm sure it doesn't justify murdering slave girls who had only carried out what their mistress had ordered. As soon as I learnt what Odysseus and Telemachus had done I left for Olympus, resolving to have nothing more to do with either of them. Penelope, still locked in her room, was not aware of how Odysseus and his son were treating her favourite servants. If she had known I'm sure she would have protested vigorously, but by the time she arrived downstairs it was all over and there just remained twelve young bodies swinging on a rope.

CHAPTER 18

ANOTHER MEETING

Hera: Welcome! Please come in, sit where you want and make yourselves comfortable. Refreshments should be here shortly. Now, first I want to congratulate both of you on your recent achievements in successfully helping your respective heroes. You, Aphrodite, for making sure your son Aeneas took over his destined role as King of Latium. And you, Athena, for leading Odysseus back to his home, and his becoming King of Ithaca again in spite of all his difficulties. Well done, both of you.

Athena: Please don't congratulate me, or call Odysseus my 'hero'. I wish I'd never met him or helped him get to Ithaca when I think of the crimes he committed when he got there.

Hera: Understood. But to change the subject I note you've both been in touch with Calliope about how to organize your life stories so that the bards can sing about you. So well done on that as well.

Aphrodite: What about you, Hera? What exactly have you achieved recently? Apart, I mean, from encouraging Turnus to pick a quite unnecessary fight against the Trojans.

Hera: Well, I did once support Jason in his quest for the

Golden Fleece in much the same way as you have supported Aeneas – though you probably don't remember that. More recently, I have arranged with Zeus that we, the gods of Greece, will continue to be worshipped in Latium, and throughout Italy. Anyway, let's not go on about the past. It's the future I invited you here to discuss. As you know, I have the gift of prophecy.

Aphrodite: A gift which doesn't seem to have helped you when it came to supporting Turnus against Aeneas.

Hera: Please, Aphrodite, can we abandon that topic. Now, as to the future, I can tell you that Greece is about to enter a dark age.

Athena: What exactly does that mean – dark age?

Hera: Mycenae will fall, trade will decline, and then one day armies from the new city of Rome will descend on us. They will conquer first Macedonia, and then the rest of the Greek world. Our land will become a bit of a colony, a backwater. But there is good news as well. The future may hold a threat, but to us immortals it also holds a challenge. We have to learn to adapt – perhaps completely change – our roles as gods and goddesses and our very names if we are to survive. So let us work together and forget old rivalries.

Athena: How do we change our roles?

Hera: The Romans are a pious lot, but they tend to lack imagination. They want wise gods whom they may respect – gods who live pure lives and are never objects of humour and ridicule – like some of us have been in the past.

Athena: Surely they already have their own gods. Why would they need any more?

Hera: Its true they do have some gods. For instance, they

have the Lares, gods of the family. Every Roman family has a little shrine in their house where they keep sacred objects to do with their ancestors, and at each meal they make offerings of food and wine to their own Lares. The Romans also have foreign gods like Mithras whom they have borrowed from other nations. Mithras was a Persian god but today Roman soldiers worship him with secret rituals and prayers.

Athena: So why do they need us?

Hera: The Romans are – or soon will be – very keen on Greek culture, which is so much older than theirs. And of course that includes us, the famous gods of Mount Olympus.

Aphrodite: Will we all have to change our roles, like you say? Do you seriously believe Zeus will change? I hardly think so.

Hera: My husband and I have already discussed this and he completely agrees with me. In Rome he will become Jupiter, the honoured and powerful leader of a new, more serious, more moral, team of gods. New temples will be built in his honour, including a huge one on the Capitoline Hill in the middle of Rome. I am also pleased to say that he has promised to respect our marriage vows, and will in future no longer spend half his time chasing nymphs and the daughters of kings.

Aphrodite: You seem to be painting a rather depressing picture of the future. All this about becoming respectable and moral.

Hera: I haven't mentioned the best bit. If we can rise to this new challenge we will all have more power and influence. The Romans are religious by nature and will be happy to worship any god whom they can truly respect. And from now on, their empire is going to get bigger and wider. So for us – if we play our cards right – there will be far more worshippers, more temples, more sacrifices than ever before.

Aphrodite: I think I'll be all right in any case. The Romans will always honour me because I brought the founder of their nation, Aeneas, to Italy from Troy.

Athena: Actually, I don't think there is much connection between Aeneas and the foundation of Rome. It's what they call 'invented history.' Wouldn't you agree, Hera?

Hera: It hasn't happened yet so let's not argue about it. But can I have another word with you, Aphrodite? It's about something that affects you much more then Athena.

Aphrodite: What is it?

Hera: You remember that time you got into bed with your lover, Ares, and then you couldn't get out again because Hephaestus had cast a net over the two of you? And all the other gods came and mocked you for it.

Aphrodite: What of it?

Hera: Two things really. First, I know you took Ares as a lover because you had lost interest in sex with your husband, Hephaestus. Well, Ares is going to become Mars, the Roman god of war, and because the Romans are so keen on war he will be number two to Jupiter in the divine pecking order. I very much doubt he will want to ruin his reputation by taking any lovers – even you – after that promotion. And second, I'm pleased to tell you Hephaestus is also going to change. He will become more handsome and lose his limp. His name will be Vulcan and he'll be the Roman god of fire, with a workshop in Sicily under Mount Etna, the volcano. So what I'm saying is: perhaps from now on you could stick to sex with your husband and not take any more lovers, okay? Oh, I nearly forgot – your Roman name is to be Venus.

Athena: And what about me in this new dispensation? Will I also need to change?

Hera: Yes and no. Your new name will be Minerva. You will still be patron goddess of Athens but you will also have a temple on the Capitoline like me and Jupiter – I'll be called Juno. So you'll be a pretty important goddess, but more of peace than war. The Romans can't allow female gods to dominate their wars. Best of luck to all three of us in the new Roman Empire! To quote a famous Roman author (yet to be born): *'Graecia capta ferum victorem cepit et artes intulit agresti Latio.'*

Athena & Aphrodite: What does that mean?

Hera: 'Conquered Greece, captured her savage conqueror and brought her arts into rustic Italy.' (Arts of course includes gods.) I'm afraid we're all going to have to learn Latin.

APPENDIX I: THE GODS

A major difference between us and the ancient Greeks, those who sat and listened while bards recited the stories that have come down to us as the *Iliad* and the *Odyssey*, was that theirs was a world full of life, of animation, in which gods played a major role. Does anyone today believe those Greek gods really existed? Of course not. We live after the Enlightenment and the scientific revolution. But did those who composed and recited these stories, and did their listeners, actually believe in the gods? Certainly. They respected them, prayed to them, built temples and shrines in their honour. They believed in their power, and were careful never to offend them. Modern editors and commentators on the epics may think that 'Divine machinery is an obsolete literary device.'[1] But does one build a temple to a literary device?

There existed all kinds of divine and semi-divine beings, ranging from the twelve Olympian gods headed by Zeus down through monsters and lesser gods and finally to the thousands of nymphs who seem to have populated every corner of the world. There were nymphs of the deep ocean, of rivers and lakes, of mountains, meadows and forests. Nymphs could interact with, and even marry, humans but their powers were limited and most of them were not immortal. To take one example, the hamadryads:

---

1 *David West, Introduction* to his translation of *The Aeneid*, Penguin Books 2003, xlii.

'The nymphs who haunt this great and holy mountain [Mount Ida] are neither mortals nor immortal Gods. Long is their life, and immortal food do they eat . . . At their birth there sprang up pine trees or tall-crested oaks. But when the fate of death approaches, first do the fair trees wither on the ground, and the bark about them moulders, and the twigs fall down, and even as the tree perishes so the soul of the nymph leaves the light of the sun.'[2]

Circe, daughter of the sun god Helios, was a nymph whom Odysseus encountered during his travels. She was also a witch who could use potions and herbs to cast her spells. She had been banished by her father to the remote island of Aeaea for using magic to turn a rival in love into the monster, Scylla. And another powerful nymph was Calypso who held Odysseus prisoner for years on another island until Zeus ordered his release. Then there was Oenone, a mountain nymph gifted in medical matters. She was the wife of Paris, who abandoned her for Helen of Troy. (For Circe and Calypso, see chapter 9; for Oenone, chapters 5 and 8.)

The twelve Olympian gods were more or less one family, all inter-related. Human rules of incest didn't apply to them. For example, Hera was Zeus's wife and also his sister. Unfortunately, the epics do not go into much detail about their personal lives. Homer was more interested in their relationship to mortals, especially to so-called heroes – almost all males, of course. We know the Olympians lived at the top of Mount Olympus, the highest mountain in Greece. In the Olympic village they each had their own hall or palace. They probably had many servants, though we

---

2 *Homeric Hymns 5; Aphrodite,* translated by Andrew Lang, 2005, 258-273.

hear nothing about them. Or perhaps the Olympic halls cleaned themselves and didn't need servants. Like the magic palace of the witch Circe on her island where 'the floor was always clean, the tables gleaming. The ashes vanished from the fireplace, the dishes washed themselves, and the firewood regrew overnight.'[3]

Most likely it was Hephaestus, the son of Hera, and his band of craftsmen who built these halls and furnished them. Using a combination of magic and his skills as a blacksmith he also made thunderbolts for Zeus, and for the mortal hero Achilles a suit of armour that no spear or arrow could penetrate. Hephaestus always responded to special requests. His smithy was just outside the village so that smoke from its fires and the noise of hammering didn't disturb the other gods. Some of his staff were Cyclopes, and others were robots which he himself had made.

What else do we know? Instead of blood, immortals had ichor coursing through their veins. Ichor was toxic to humans; it was said even a single drop could kill a man. The food of the gods was ambrosia and their drink, nectar. We do not know what the ingredients of either were, but both may have contained fermented honey, or mead. Whatever nectar and ambrosia were made of they must have constituted a repetitive and restricted diet which was perhaps why gods enjoyed eating human food whenever they were invited to a feast in the world down below. When a new god, Dionysus, requested to join the Olympians he was welcomed by all except the puritan Hera because he was the inventor of wine. It seems that from then on, wine instead of mead became the main ingredient of nectar, by popular choice.

---

3 Madeline Miller, *Circe*, Bloomsbury Publishing 2019, 69.

Gods had certain abilities but didn't require the drudgery of learning. Athena was born holding a spear and wearing a helmet. She hardly needed to acquire the skills of warfare because she knew them from the start. Aphrodite, goddess of love and beauty, understood the arts of seduction without having been taught them. The Olympians had other divine powers, such as the ability to transport themselves rapidly across land and sea. Hermes, messenger of the gods, with his winged sandals and winged helmet, was particularly good at this, but they all could do it. Another skill, useful on the battlefield, was the ability to hide themselves in a thick mist so that they were invisible. And then there was the power to disguise themselves to look like someone else. One problem associated with this must have been the danger that the mortal chosen might actually turn up. For example, when Athena took on the likeness of Mentor, an old friend of Odysseus, a passing human became suspicious:

'I saw Mentor embark as captain – or perhaps
not Mentor but a god who looked like him.
This puzzles me, that yesterday at dawn
I saw great Mentor here, though he had gone
to Pylos in the ship.'[4]

A god might also transform a mortal to look like someone else. This was perhaps a skill which some Olympians tended to over-use. For instance, one can quite see why Athena changed Odysseus into a wrinkled old beggar so as to avoid danger when he first arrived back home in Ithaca after many years abroad (see chapter 17), but why did Aphrodite need to turn herself into a young

---

4 *The Odyssey*, book 4, 653-658, translated by Emily Wilson, Norton Critical Editions, 2020.

local girl out hunting when she wanted to explain to Aeneas about the kingdom of Dido where he had just landed? Couldn't she have done this just as well as herself? She was his mother after all, and in fact Aeneas did recognise her in spite of the disguise. (See chapter 10.)

Certain gods – Hera, for instance – could see into the future, an ability that one or two mortals, such as Tiresias the Greek and Hellenus, the Trojan prince, also possessed. Not that seeing into the future helped Hera much since she seems to have spent much of her energy trying to avoid what she knew had been ordained by the Fates! The Fates were three old women who sat round the fire in a cave somewhere in the world. One spun out the thread of the life of a mortal, another measured its length, and the third decided when to cut it. And no god could prevent what the Fates had decreed – though sometimes it does seem uncertain whether Zeus or the Fates had the last word.[5]

Zeus was King of the Olympian gods, and therefore of the entire world, but even so there were limits to his power. Nor was he keen on doing something that all the other gods opposed. For instance, towards the end of the Trojan war, when all the gods were watching Achilles chasing Hector, and about to kill him, Zeus spoke out: *'Oh, I love this man who is being pursued around the walls [of Troy]. My heart is saddened for Hector . . . Well then, give thought to it, gods, and consider whether we shall save him from death.'*

Then Athena came out with: *'Father, what is this you are saying? Do you intend to take a man who is mortal and long ago doomed by fate, and release him from grim death?*

---

5 Robert Graves, *The Greek Myths*, Penguin Books 1992, 48.

Do it then, but we other gods will not approve you.[6]

Zeus was moved by this reply, and Hector was allowed to die – not in a fair fight incidentally, but having been tricked by Athena herself. (See chapter 7.)

Sometimes Zeus would call a meeting in his palace which all the Olympians were supposed to attend. And occasionally his wife too held a meeting – for selected colleagues. Also, there were rare ceremonies to which everyone was invited, even lesser gods and nymphs. One of these was the wedding of the sea-goddess, Thetis, to the mortal, King Peleus (they became the parents of Achilles). Otherwise, life was one long holiday. There was not much to do on Olympia, and boredom must have been an ever-present threat. If you are immortal how do you fill up your time? You yourself do not change. Very soon after they were born gods became fully mature, although still youthful, and they stayed that way.

'I thought once that gods are the opposite of death, but I see now they are more dead than anything, for they are unchanging, and can hold nothing in their hands.'[7]

Luckily for the gods there were mortals living down below with whom they could get involved and play with – if they moved fast. A human had such a short life. Also that life was always changing. One minute they were babies, then children, then grown-ups, and not long after that they became too old to accomplish anything worthwhile. And then they died – of course they might also die at any point in their lives, from birth onwards. But gods stayed the way they were, youthful but mature. It was hard for humans to

6 *The Iliad,* book 22, 176-184, trans. by David West, Penguin Classics, 1987.

7 Madeline Miller, *Circe,* 333.

understand the nature of divine immortality. There is a story which shows that it could be difficult even for gods themselves to grasp what living for ever actually meant. Eos was a goddess, though not an Olympian. She is sometimes called Lady Dawn because her task was to bring in the dawn every morning. One day Eos fell deeply in love with a handsome young mortal named Tithonus, but she could never stop herself from worrying about how one day he would die. So she went to see Zeus and begged him to give her lover immortality, to which he surprised her by immediately agreeing.

'*Is there anything else you would like to ask me for, Eos?*'

'*Oh no, heavenly father. And Tithonus and I will be eternally grateful to you for this gift.*'

The rest of this story is rather pathetic. At first they were the happiest and most beautiful young couple in the world. But gradually Tithonus showed signs of ageing. He started to stoop and his hair went grey. Back went Eos to Zeus and complained, but he pointed out she had never asked for him to have eternal youth, only immortality. Finally, when Tithonus became so old that he could neither walk nor speak, and wanted only to die, Eos was forced to turn him into a grasshopper – presumably an immortal one.

The relationship between a human and a god was always one-sided since gods were so much more powerful. When Achilles showed sympathy for Priam who was begging for the release of his dead son Hector's body, he said to Priam: '*No good can come from chilling tears. This is the fate the gods have spun for poor mortal men, that we should live in misery, but they themselves have no sorrows.* [8]

Gods could help mortals achieve their ambitions, or they could punish, even kill them. They could send down a plague to destroy a whole city or they could help a new city to be built. They liked humans who respected them, prayed to them, sacrificed animals to them, and they favoured cities where there was a temple dedicated to themselves. They also often gave their support to certain elite leaders, some of whom actually had divine parentage (Hercules was a son of Zeus; Achilles, a son of Thetis). But mortals whom they thought didn't treat them properly, or boasted that they were superior to them in some way, often received brutal punishment. Marsyas, a satyr, once claimed to be a better musician than Apollo. A contest was held which Apollo won, and then the god, usually so reasonable and charming, killed his opponent by flaying the skin off him. In another story Arachne, a simple peasant girl, told her friends she was a better weaver than Athena, who in revenge turned her into a spider.

A god might spend hours looking after a particular human favourite and protecting them from danger on the battlefield, or as they sailed across the sea. When night fell and the fighting ceased, or the ship anchored, the god could return to Mount Olympus and resume his or her watch the following morning. Many Olympian gods – though not Aphrodite – particularly enjoyed human wars where they could choose to lend their support to one side or the other. Being immortal, they themselves couldn't be killed, though they could be injured and this might cause them great pain. Nevertheless, the wound would soon heal itself. Typically, during a battle a god or goddess might render themselves

---

8 *Iliad,* book 24, 526-28.

invisible and stand beside whichever hero they had decided to help, using their powers to deflect any enemy arrow or spear that looked like reaching its target. Aeneas, the Trojan leader, once said, *'It is not possible for any man to fight against Achilles – there is always one of the gods at his side to keep him from destruction.'*[9]

One of the reasons why a god might decide to support a particular mortal was because they were playing a game of rivalry with other gods. It usually had little to do with what we would call morality.

These Olympians were then not at all like the Christian god that succeeded them. In the words of Emily Wilson: *'The gods in The Odyssey, like those of The Iliad*[10] *are self-interested beings, whose interventions in human lives are motivated primarily by their own desires, whims, and preferences rather than by a consistent commitment to uphold moral law.'*[11]

This is even true of Zeus, though in his case he did at least support the principle of *xenia*, whereby all visitors, and especially the poor and the homeless, had to be welcomed to a household and shown hospitality.

To sum up: gods and mortals were interlocked in a symbiotic relationship. Mortals needed the gods to listen to their prayers and help them when help was required. Gods needed mortals to give their own lives a sense of purpose, and also they somehow became more powerful when they were widely worshipped (see chapter 2 for Athena's surge of power after she became the patron goddess of Athens).

---

9 *Iliad,* book 20, 95.

10 And we might add here *The Aeneid.*

11 In the introduction to her translation of *The Odyssey*, xxvii-viii.

But did the interference of gods and goddesses in the life of mortals reduce human free will? For a discussion on this question see Appendix II.

APPENDIX II: FREE WILL

One issue lurking behind the divine narratives in this book, as well as in the ancient epics, is that of human free will. If the gods and goddesses of Olympia were so powerful that they could direct human beings, what does this say about the free will of the Greek and Roman mortals who feature in these epics? Did they believe they could make their own choices? And how credible is our own conviction that we have free will? In this appendix I look at what the Greek and Roman epics have to say about free will, and then briefly compare this with what certain philosophers and neurophysicists think about that topic today.

To start with the epics, one has to remember that these consist of lively narratives about the adventures of certain 'heroes'; their authors spend little time discussing theoretical problems such as free will. And even when such issues do crop up, the conclusions are not always clear. For instance, when Aeneas decides to leave Dido he tells her, '*It is not by my own will that I search for Italy.*'[12]

This probably means, not that the Fates or the gods are forcing him to go to Italy but rather that he feels he has a duty to go there which he is choosing to live up to rather than staying in Carthage with her. But even here there is a sense that mortals like Aeneas felt that they were being put

---

12 *Aeneid*, book 4, 361.

under pressure to take certain decisions – possibly against their own personal desires.

I'd like to give a few clearer examples of such pressure felt by mortals, and imposed on them by forces stronger than themselves. My quotes are mainly taken from the *Iliad* where free will is mentioned more than in either the *Odyssey* or the *Aeneid* since the story concerns the Trojan war in which the gods frequently participated, and when they did, human free will came under threat.

EXAMPLES OF NO FREE WILL

(1) When Menelaus decided to challenged Hector to single combat he said: 'I myself shall arm against this man [although] the threads of victory are not in our hands, they are held above, among the immortal gods.'[13]

(2) 'I am not to blame,' said Agamemnon after he had ended his quarrel with Achilles, 'but rather Zeus and [the Fates] … they put a cruel blindness in my mind at the assembly on that day when by my own act I took away his prize from Achilles. But what could I do? It is a god who brings all things to their end.' [14]

(3) When discussing the fatal decision of Patroclus to pursue the Trojans right up to the walls of Troy, Homer comments: 'Zeus's mind is always stronger than the mind of men – he can bring terror on even the brave man and easily rid him of victory: and then again he himself will spur a man to fight. And it was Zeus then who put the urge in Patroclus's heart.'[15]

---

13 *Iliad*, book 7, 98-100.
14 *Iliad*, book 19, 86-90.
15 *Iliad*, book 16, 87-90.

In other words, it was Zeus who made Patroclus disobey the order which Achilles had given him not to advance towards the Trojan walls.

My next two examples are slightly different. They show physical actions by gods which overrule human attempts to exert their own freedom of choice. But for the mortal concerned the result was just the same – no free will.

(4) At various moments in the war, it was Athena who repeatedly caused a spear to find its human target, or alternatively deflected a well-directed spear away from whoever she happened to be protecting at the time.

(5) If necessary a god could even remove their client from the fighting and carry him to a place of safety. When Aphrodite realised that Paris was about to be killed by Menelaus she snatched him from the battlefield, 'wrapped him in thick mist, and set him down in his sweetly scented bedroom [in Troy].'[16]

(6) A final, rather picturesque, example is from the *Aeneid*. Hera orders the Fury, Alecto, to infect the sleeping Turnus with a fever for war against the Trojans (see chapter 15): 'She threw a burning torch at the warrior and it lodged deep in his heart smoking with black light. A great terror burst in upon his sleep, and the sweat broke out all over his body and soaked him to the bone. In a frenzy of rage he roared for his armour … the lust for battle raged within him, the criminal madness of war.'[17]

EXAMPLES OF DOUBLE MOTIVATION

Often, however, the text implies that even without the god's

---

16 *Iliad*, book 3, 79-81.
17 *Aeneid*, book 7, 457-463.

intervention the brave hero might have achieved the same result. This was 'double motivation', a way of reconciling human free will with divine power. Here are some examples, the first again taken from the *Iliad*.

(1) Aeneas explains that Achilles' skills as a warrior are such that he hardly needs divine help. If he chose, he could achieve the same result on his own: 'It is not possible, then, for any man to fight against Achilles – there is always one of the gods at his side to keep him from destruction. And even without that, his spear flies straight, and never stops until it has passed through a man's flesh.'[18]

(2) Another example is from the *Odyssey* when the hero is nearly drowned after Poseidon wrecks his boat. Through skill and sheer will power Odysseus was able to swim for two days and nights before being cast up on the shore of an unknown island. But the text also tells us that he was helped throughout this trauma by no less than three gods. There was Ino, the White Goddess, who gave him a magic scarf which would prevent him from drowning; Athena, who smoothed the waves in front of him as he swam; and finally an unnamed river god who showed him a safe place to land at the mouth of his river.[19]

(3) One of the most obvious examples of double motivation comes from the *Aeneid* when Dido first met – and seemed at once to fall in love with – Aeneas. But Aphrodite, who always watched over and protected her son, felt she could not be sure how strong this human attraction was or how long it might last. After all, Aeneas and his fellow Trojans were vulnerable strangers in a foreign city. So she wanted to make sure. She ordered her

---

18 *Iliad*, book 20, 94-97.
19 *Odyssey*, book 5, 314-457.

son Eros to shoot one of his magic arrows at Dido in order to infect her heart with the true madness of love. [20]

PROPHECIES AND PORTENTS

Do the frequent prophecies and portents that occur throughout the epics, especially in the *Aeneid*, invalidate free will? Sometimes prophecies don't change anything; for example, those of Cassandra because everyone ignores them. Sometimes they are so vague, especially as regards time, that they allow initial disobedience, for example, Zeus's prophesy that Aeneas would one day reach the river Tiber. The efforts of Poseidon and Hera succeed in delaying this forecast for years. Sometimes the prophecy involves two alternative futures; for example, when Hellenus tells Odysseus he can reach Ithaca with his followers, but only if they refrain from killing the cattle of the sun god Helios on the way. Likewise, portents – a sign in the sky, a flight of birds, a voice from the depth of the forest heard by King Latinus advising him not to give his daughter in marriage to Turnus – all these, like prophecies, tend to influence, but not to determine, the freely made decisions of those who saw or heard them.

IN BATTLE

There are times when the protagonist involved in battle seems possessed by an irrational madness which stops him thinking rationally. For instance, when Achilles fought to avenge the death of Patroclus he became 'a man in full fury' who 'stormed with his spear all over the field like some

---

20 *Odyssey,* book 1, 680-690.

inhuman being, driving men on and killing them: and the black earth ran with blood.'[21] Or Aeneas who, 'burning with mad passion and terrible in his wrath', killed his enemy Turnus when he was begging for mercy.[22] Neither of them required Alecto to infect them (see above). At such moments rational thought and hence free will seem to vanish. Such cases may not always be due to the intervention of a god, but they do signal that these heroes are not in control at the time.

CONCLUSION

Characters in the epics believe they generally have free will but they also realise that they are restricted by what the Fates or Zeus may have chosen for them. In each concrete scenario, human actors understand that they are independent only within limits, if at all. Sometimes they may find themselves choosing to act in tandem with a god (that is, double motivation). In all cases, they must be careful not to offend divine beings who are so much more powerful than they are.

'This is absurd, that mortals blame the gods!' says Zeus. 'They say we cause their suffering, but they themselves increase it by folly.

He cites the example of Aegisthus who seduced Agamemnon's wife when the latter was away fighting in the war. When Agamemnon returned from Troy Aegisthus killed him even though he'd been warned not to by Zeus himself via his messenger, Hermes. Mortals may act on their own free will but their wicked actions will be

---

21 *Iliad*, book 20, 493-495.
22 *Aeneid*, book 12, 953.

observed by the gods and perhaps punished:

Aegisthus would not hear that good advice.
But now his death has paid all debts.[23]

TODAY

Over millennia the accepted view has been that we do have free will and consequently are responsible for our own decisions. The institutions of our cultures and societies are based on this assumption. But it is also true that Christian theologians and those of other faiths have had great difficulty over the centuries in reconciling human free will with divine omniscience. Part of their solution to this problem has often been to say that God is outside of time, and therefore that past, present and future are all one to him. A human, who lives in time, might have free will but viewed from the larger context of divine knowledge it disappears – not an easy concept to grasp!

In recent decades, however, many philosophers and scientists in the West have started to question the very existence of free will, calling it an 'inherently flawed and incoherent concept', and an 'anachronistic myth rendered obsolete by the power of modern science to know us better than we know ourselves'.[24] One reason for this view is that neuroscientists are now beginning to be able to scan the brain and observe the chains of neurons firing their messages. It turns out that people's desires and decisions – our so-called free choices – can be predicted before we

---

23 *Odyssey,* book 1, 31-44.

24 Oliver Burkeman, *The clockwork universe: is free will an illusion?* The Guardian, 27 Apr 2021. See also Sam Harris, *Free Will,* Free Press, 2012.

ourselves become aware of them. In other words, the choices made by our conscious minds have been dictated by previous events in our brains of which we were unconscious.

At this stage I want to bring in Thomas Metzinger, a leading philosopher of the mind, who has used the metaphor of an ego tunnel to describe the limits of our conscious experience: *What we see and hear, or what we feel and smell and taste, is only a small fraction of what actually exists out there. Our conscious model of reality is a low-dimensional projection of the inconceivably richer physical reality surrounding and sustaining us ... Therefore, the on-going process of conscious experience is not so much an image of reality as a tunnel through reality.*

The reason I quote Metzinger is because his ego-tunnel metaphor suggests that it might actually be impossible for us – educated modern westerners – to perceive reality in the same way as other earlier human cultures may have perceived it. If true, this would have some bearing on our attitude to an ancient world in which nymphs and gods mingled freely with humans. I quote a passage from his chapter entitled 'The Appearance of a World': *Human beings in other historical epochs – during the Vedic period of ancient India, say, or during the European Middle Ages, when God was still perceived as a real and constant presence – likely knew kinds of subjective experience almost inaccessible to us today. Many deep forms of conscious self-experience have become all but impossible due to philosophical enlightenment and the rise of science and technology – at least for the many millions of well-educated, scientifically informed people. Theories change social practice, and practice eventually changes brains, the way we perceive the world.*[25]

For the heroes of the epics, to encounter a god or a nymph during their travels was perhaps surprising but quite possible. However, for us, according to Metzinger, it would be inconceivable – in the literal sense of the word. When Odysseus crept exhausted onto an unknown beach after swimming across the sea for two days and nights, he found a good place to sleep near the bank of a river mouth (see chapter 14).

The next morning something woke him up. 'What is this country I have come to now?' he asked himself.

'I heard the sound of female voices. Is it
nymphs, who frequent the craggy mountain tops,
and river streams and meadows lush with grass?
Or could this noise I hear be human voices?
I have to try to find out who they are.'[26]

It was young Nausicaa and her servants playing a ball game. They weren't nymphs but they could easily have been.

'Hold on,' you might say, 'Odysseus couldn't ever have seen a nymph because they don't exist and never have.'

'Well, colours don't exist either,' a neuroscientist might reply, 'our brains invent them as we go along. Yet they seem real enough to us.'

To sum up on free will: there seems to be a kind of correspondence between us and the ancient Greeks. In the epics the human characters believed – in theory – that they

---

25 This and the previous passage are from Thomas Metzinger, *The Ego Tunnel*, Basic Books, 2009, pp. 7 & 17. I am worried that these two brief excerpts may merely confuse the reader, and don't do any justice to Metzinger's thoughts. If you feel confused, please acquire the book!

26 *Odyssey*, book 6, 119-126.

possessed it, but in practice it was governed by beings more powerful than themselves. Today, again, most people tend to assume free will exists, but if we accept the recent advances in neuroscience, it really doesn't! We are at the mercy of psycho-biological processes of which we are usually ignorant. Like the characters in Homer, and in fact like all of humanity, we – that is, our conscious selves – are not in control. The difference, perhaps, between us and those ancient Greek warriors is that they understood this whereas we in the modern West are ignorant of it. We live and love – and die – mistakenly believing that we are the sole actors in our own epics.

A NOTE ON SOURCES AND THE AUTHOR

My sources are mainly *The Iliad*, *The Odyssey*, and Virgil's *Aeneid*. For these I have used the following translations: Martin Hammond, *The Iliad*, Penguin Books 1987.

Emily Wilson, *The Odyssey*, W.W. Norton & Company 2020.

David West, *The Aeneid*, Penguin Books 2003.

Many novels have recently been published which expand or elaborate on selected episodes from the epics, and I have also borrowed a few ideas from these. They include:

Margaret Atwood, *The Penelopiad*, Canongate Books 2018

Amanda Elyot, *The Memoirs of Helen of Troy*, Crown Publishers, New York 2005

Stephen Fry, *Mythos*, Penguin Books 2018 & *Troy*, Penguin Books 2021

Adèle Geras, *Dido*, David Fickling Books 2010

Natalie Haynes, *A Thousand Ships*, Picador 2020

Daphne Ignatius, *My Life as Athena*, Concertia Press, Roswell, Georgia 2014

Ursula Le Guin, *Lavinia*, Weidenfeld & Nicolson 2010

Madeline Miller, *Circe*, Bloomsbury Publishing 2019

Also useful have been:

Robert Graves, *The Greek Myths*, Penguin Books 1992

Carl Kerenyi, *The Gods of the Greeks*, Thames and Hudson 1979

A word on the cover: the three birds used on the cover and at chapter headings in the book were chosen as their own symbols by the three goddesses themselves. The owl for Athena; the dove for Aphrodite; the peacock for Hera.

A word about footnotes: There are footnotes in my appendices, but otherwise not. I presume the goddesses didn't believe in them so I didn't put them in. And one final point – about the names of the goddesses themselves. In order to keep things simple I have kept their Greek names throughout (Aphrodite, Athena and Hera) rather than switching to their Latin names (Venus, Minerva and Juno) when I use material taken from Virgil.

Finally, a word about me: I am a retired History teacher and lecturer living in North Yorkshire, with degrees in History from Cambridge and the University of East Anglia. I have taught at various institutions, including colleges of further education and the Open University. My last post before I retired was as Head of History at a large sixth form college. I now spend my days writing, reading and researching my areas of interest.